Samuel French Acting Edition

Fly By Night

Conceived by Kim Rosenstock

Written by Will Connolly,
Michael Mitnick &
Kim Rosenstock

SAMUELFRENCH.COM   SAMUELFRENCH.CO.UK

FOR PRODUCTION ENQUIRIES

UNITED STATES AND CANADA
Info@SamuelFrench.com
1-866-598-8449

UNITED KINGDOM AND EUROPE
Plays@SamuelFrench.co.uk
020-7255-4302

Each title is subject to availability from Samuel French, depending upon country of performance. Please be aware that FLY BY NIGHT may not be licensed by Samuel French in your territory. Professional and amateur producers should contact the nearest Samuel French office or licensing partner to verify availability.

MUSIC USE NOTE

Licensees are solely responsible for obtaining formal written permission from copyright owners to use copyrighted music in the performance of this play and are strongly cautioned to do so. If no such permission is obtained by the licensee, then the licensee must use only original music that the licensee owns and controls. Licensees are solely responsible and liable for all music clearances and shall indemnify the copyright owners of the play(s) and their licensing agent, Samuel French, against any costs, expenses, losses and liabilities arising from the use of music by licensees. Please contact the appropriate music licensing authority in your territory for the rights to any incidental music.

RENTAL MATERIALS

An orchestration consisting of

- **Piano/Conductor score (Used for rehearsals and performance)**
- **Drums**
- **Guitar**
- **Bass**
- **7 Vocal Chorus Books**

will be loaned two months prior to the production ONLY on the receipt of the Licensing Fee quoted for all performances, the rental fee and a refundable deposit. Please contact Samuel French for perusal of the music materials as well as a performance license application.

IMPORTANT BILLING AND CREDIT REQUIREMENTS

If you have obtained performance rights to this title, please refer to your licensing agreement for important billing and credit requirements.

FLY BY NIGHT was first produced by TheatreWorks (Robert Kelley, Artistic Director; Phil Santora, Managing Director; Meredith McDonough, Director of New Works) in Palo Alto, CA on July 13, 2011. The performance was directed by Bill Fennelly, with sets by Dane Laffrey, costumes by Tanya Finkelstein, lights by Paul Toben, sound by Jeff Mockus, musical staging by Kikau Alvaro, dramaturgy by Meredith McDonough, and music direction and orchestrations by Mike Pettry. The Production Stage Manager was Jamie D. Mann. The cast was as follows:

NARRATOR...................................Wade McCollum

HAROLD MCCLAM................................Ian Leonard

MR. MCCLAM ....James Judy

DAPHNE ....Rachel Spencer Hewitt

MIRIAM... Kristin Stokes

CRABBLE...................................Michael McCormick

JOEY STORMS...................................... Keith Pinto

FLY BY NIGHT was subsequently produced at Dallas Theatre Center (Kevin Moriarty, Artistic Director, Heather M. Kitchen, Managing Director) in Texas on April 26, 2013. The performance was directed by Bill Fennelly, with sets by Dane Laffrey, costumes by Paloma H. Young, lights by Paul Toben, sound by Zachary Williamson, choreography by Joel Ferrell, dramaturgy by Meredith McDonough, and musical direction by Zak Sandler. The Production Stage Manager was Monica A Cuoco. The band was Foe Destroyer: Chris McQueen, guitar; Daniel Garcia, bass; Cade Sadler, percussion. The cast was as follows:

NARRATOR....................................... Asa Somers

HAROLD MCCLAM.............................. Damon Daunno

MR. MCCLAM ....David Coffee

DAPHNE .... Whitney Bashor

MIRIAM... Kristin Stokes

CRABBLE...................................Michael McCormick

JOEY STORMS...................................... Alex Organ

FLY BY NIGHT receieved its New York premiere at Playwrights Horizons (Tim Sanford, Artistic Director; Leslie Marcus, Managing Director; Kent Nicholson, Director of Musical Theater) on May 16, 2014. The performance was directed by Carolyn Cantor, with sets by David Korins, costumes by Paloma Young, lights by Jeff Croiter, sound by Ken Travis and Alex Hawthorn, choreography by Sam Pinkleton, and musical direction by Vadim Feichtner. The Production Stage Manager was Kyle Gates. The band was Foe Destroyer: Chris McQueen, guitar; Daniel Garcia, bass; Cade Sadler, percussion. The cast was as follows:

NARRATOR . . . . Henry Stram

HAROLD MCCLAM . . . . .Adam Chanler-Berat

MR. MCCLAM . . . . .Peter Friedman

DAPHNE . . . . Patti Murin

MIRIAM . . . ., ...Allison Case

CRABBLE . . . . Michael McCormick

JOEY STORMS . . . . Bryce Ryness

FLY BY NIGHT was first developed and presented by Yale Summer Cabaret, 2009 (Kim Rosenstock, Artistic Director; Whitney Estrin, Managing Director).

FLY BY NIGHT received a workshop production as part of TheatreWorks' New Works Festival, 2010 (Meredith Mcdonough, Director of New Works) .

FLY BY NIGHT received a workshop at The American Musical Theatre Project at Northwestern University, 2011.

FLY BY NIGHT received a workshop at Roundabout Theatre Company, 2012.

CHARACTERS

NARRATOR – our guide
HAROLD MCCLAM – a sandwich maker
MR. MCCLAM – a father
DAPHNE – an actress
MIRIAM – a waitress
CRABBLE – a deli owner
JOEY STORMS – a playwright

TIME

1964 – 1965

SETTING

New York City
(with the occasional detour to South Dakota)

FLASH MOMENTS

This story jumps around in time. In order to help navigate the time-line, there are certain key moments in the story that get revisited in flash moments. These flashes are intended to be visual and narrative signposts for the audience, and therefore it's important they appear the same each time they occur.

SPEECH NOTE

A slash (/) in a sentence indicates where the next line begins to overlap with it.

STAGING NOTE

While many different locations are visited in the show, only the essential elements should be depicted onstage to allow for the rhythm and fluidity of the storytelling to remain intact.

NOTE ON TONE AND THE NARRATOR

This musical is a dark comedy. Striking the right balance in tone is crucial to the overall impact of the piece. The humor – especially the Narrator's – is intended to be dry and should not be played broadly. The darker moments should be handled truthfully without tipping into the overly sentimental.

The Narrator weaves in and out of the story, transforming into many different characters along the way. These transformations should be achieved as seamlessly as possible and without fanfare. While playfulness is encouraged, lots of props and extra costume pieces are not necessary. We found that more nuanced shifts in voice and physicality did the trick. Of course, the occasional prop was used. And, for what it's worth, the Gypsy almost always wore a headscarf.

MUSICAL NUMBERS

ACT ONE

Prologue
"Fly By Night".................................... **COMPANY**

Scene One – Harold
"Circles in the Sand" .... **HAROLD** and **BAND**

Scene Two – Daphne
"Daphne Dreams" .... **DAPHNE** and **NARRATOR**

Scene Three – Harold & Daphne
"More Than Just a Friend" .... **HAROLD** and **DAPHNE**

Scene Four – Miriam
"Stars, I Trust" .... **MIRIAM**

"Breakfast All Day"........................ **MIRIAM** and **CHORUS**

Scene Five – Mr. McClam and His Record Player (Part 1)

Scene Six – Joey
"What You Do To Me" .... **JOEY STORMS** and **DAPHNE**

"More Than Just a Friend (Reprise)".................... **HAROLD**

Scene Seven – The Prophecy
"The Prophecy" .... **NARRATOR, MIRIAM** and **CHORUS**

"Diner" .... **HAROLD** and **MIRIAM**

Scene Eight – The Triangle
"Circles in the Sand (Reprise)"........................ **HAROLD**

ACT TWO

Scene One – The Middle
"Pulled Apart" .... **MIRIAM**

"Eternity" .... **HAROLD** and **CRABBLE**

Scene Two – Mr. McClam and His Record Player (Part 2)

Scene Three – The Rut

Scene Four – A New Ending
"I Need More" ....**DAPHNE**

Scene Five – The Break
"At Least I'll Know I Tried"........................... **COMPANY**

Scene Six – The Train Station
"Me With You" .... **HAROLD** and **MIRIAM**

Scene Seven – Time Stops

Scene Eight – The Blackout
"Cecily Smith"................................. **MR. MCCLAM**

Scene Nine – The Great Fall
"Fly By Night (Reprise)" .... **COMPANY**

"November Stars"............... **HAROLD, DAPHNE** and **CHORUS**

ACKNOWLEDGMENTS

Fly By Night exists because of the hard work and dedication of all the brilliant people listed on the previous pages. The authors would like to thank each and every one of them for lending their hearts and minds to the creation of this musical.

In addition, we would like to thank all of the people not listed – the actors and musicians who lent their astonishing talents to the various readings and workshops along the way, the wonderful assistants who kept things running with humor and grace, the superhuman backstage crews who saved the day over and over again, and the incredible artistic and production staffs at The 2009 Yale Summer Cabaret, TheatreWorks, Dallas Theater Center and Playwrights Horizons.

And a very special thank you to Derek Zasky – agent, friend, accidental therapist and exceptional human.

ACT ONE

PROLOGUE

*(***NARRATOR*** enters. He talks to the audience.)*

NARRATOR. I never know where to begin...

The map of this story is both tiny and vast. And beginning is as simple and complex as choosing a path to travel and trusting that it will connect to all other paths.

I suppose I could begin by telling you that there is an invisible world woven into the fabric of our daily lives. Don't go looking for this invisible world. Because you won't find it.

Because it's invisible.

Of course, it probably makes sense to begin with what we can see. Like the people. I could begin with the people.

*(The rest of the ***COMPANY*** enters.)*

[MUSIC #1: "FLY BY NIGHT"]

These are the people!

Or I could begin with the time and place:
Our story spans one year from November 9th, 1964 to November 9th, 1965.
In New York City.

OR I could begin with the structure:
Our tale tonight circles around a triangle composed of two women.

(**MIRIAM** *and* **DAPHNE** *step forward*)

NARRATOR. *(cont.)* And one man.

(**HAROLD** *steps forward.*)

But, this being a musical story and all, we should probably begin with the guitar. And in order to reach the guitar, we must first attend a funeral.

(All exit except for **MR. MCCLAM** *and* **HAROLD.***)*

On November 9th, 1964, deep in the outer reaches of Brooklyn, New York, Cecily Smith, wife and mother, passes away in her sleep when her heart stops. For days her widowed husband can't take his hand off his own heart. He presses on it and says her name.

MR. MCCLAM. *(quietly)* Cecily…

NARRATOR. At the hospital. At home. On the walk to the cemetery.

(**HAROLD** *and* **MR. MCCLAM** *walk to the cemetery.*)

NARRATOR.

LONG WIDE STRETCHES OF THE ORDINARY
SPINNING CIRCLES AS THIS LIFE ROLLS ON
FROM THE CRADLE TO THE CEMETERY
JUST GET THROUGH UNTIL TOMORROW'S DAWN

NARRATOR.	**CHORUS.**
THEN, A BURST – A	THEN – AH
SOARING PEAK, A	
SUDDEN DROP	
BEST, OR WORST – DON'T	BEST – AH
LET IT END, PLEASE	
MAKE IT STOP	
INSTANTS, MOMENTS –	

NARRATOR.

ONE FLICKERING FLAME OF LIGHT –

NARRATOR & CHORUS.

MMMMMM…

NARRATOR. Father and son stand at the gravesite.

MR. MCCLAM. *(hand on heart)* Cecily…

NARRATOR. This is Mr. McClam.

HAROLD. Dad?

NARRATOR. And this is his son, Harold.

HAROLD. Dad, they wanna know if you're ready.

(After a beat, **HAROLD** *nods for the coffin to be lowered.)*

NARRATOR. As the rain falls, they watch the coffin sink below the Earth's surface.
WHAT IS ENDLESS, WHAT IS MOMENTARY?
GRASPING MEM'RIES THAT REFUSE TO STAY

NARRATOR & CHORUS.
LONG WIDE STRETCHES OF THE ORDINARY

NARRATOR, CHORUS, JOEY.
LONG WIDE STRETCHES TAKE THEM DAY BY DAY

NARRATOR.	**CHORUS**.
THEN A BURST – THE FABRIC'S TORN BEFORE THE EYES	THEN A BURST – AH

NARRATOR & CHORUS.
BLESSED OR CURSED – THE CHILD'S BORN, THE PARENT DIES
INSTANTS, MOMENTS –
A FLICKERING, FLY-BY-NIGHT SIGHT

NARRATOR & CHORUS.
MMMMMM...

NARRATOR. After returning home, the two men sit on their stoop, watching cars.

MR. MCCLAM. You buy a new coat?

HAROLD. Yeah.

MR. MCCLAM. Looks warm.

HAROLD. It's wool.

NARRATOR. Eventually, they go inside to sort through Cecily's belongings. And deep in the shadows of her closet, behind a heavy curtain of dresses, Mr. McClam discovers an old record.

*(***MR. MCCLAM*** *holds up a record.)*

MR. MCCLAM. *La Traviata*!

    LIBIAMO, LIBIAMO NE'LIETI

    (to **HAROLD***)* Did we ever tell you about *La / Traviata?*

HAROLD. Yes. / Many times.

MR. MCCLAM. The war was over, I was living with my folks –

HAROLD. Not now, Dad.

NARRATOR.

    TRAPPING YOURSELF, WHEN YOU KNOW YOU SHOULD RUN

    MAPPING OUT WAYS, BUT NOT FOLLOWING ONE

    SCRAPPING ALL HOPE WHEN YOU'VE ONLY BEGUN

    Harold pushes his way through a mountain of dusty
    boxes filled with yellowed papers, and discovers –

    *(***HAROLD*** holds up a guitar.)*

HAROLD. *(to himself)* A guitar? *(to* **MR. MCCLAM***)* Mom had a
    guitar?

MR. MCCLAM. *(remembering)* Yes!

HAROLD. Did she play?

MR. MCCLAM. No! But she always wanted to learn.

    *(***HAROLD*** plucks the strings.)*

HAROLD. Can I have this?

MR. MCCLAM. Sure.

NARRATOR. Harold bids his father goodbye, and walks
    fifteen blocks to a bus to a train to another train that
    will take him home to his fifth-floor walk-up apartment
    in Manhattan.

    And while Mr. McClam sits at home playing his wife's
    record…

    Harold sits at home playing his mother's guitar.

    *(***HAROLD*** plays one note over and over.)*

    And less than five months later…

    (The space transforms into a night club.)

    Harold finds himself onstage in a small, smoky club,
    being introduced by an Emcee:

    (The **NARRATOR** *assumes the role of the* **EMCEE***.)*

NARRATOR/EMCEE.

Ladies and gentlemen! This guy!

(**HAROLD** *nervously approaches a microphone.*)

NARRATOR.

INSTANTS, MOMENTS –
ONE FLICKERING FLAME OF LIGHT

ALL.

MMMMMM…

Scene 1.
Harold

(HAROLD tentatively greets the audience.)

HAROLD. Hello.

NARRATOR/EMCEE. *(to HAROLD)* Ya got *three* minutes!

HAROLD. *(to audience)* Uh. My name is Harold.
I'll tell you a little about me.
I was born and raised in Brooklyn, New York!
(no response) Thank you!
I make sandwiches for a living.
And I'm going to play a song I wrote about my favorite animal: the sea turtle.
There's a beach in Florida where sea turtles nested for ages.
And when their babies were born, instinct would kick in and they'd look for the light on the horizon to guide them towards the ocean.
But then a highway was built along the beach and it needed to be lit up.
And next thing you know – the turtles are hatching and crawling toward the wrong brightness.
The wrong horizon.
The point is... I think I might be a sea turtle.

(NARRATOR/EMCEE tries to take away the mic.)

NARRATOR/EMCEE. That's it man, you're done.

HAROLD. No, wait! I'm about to play. Where was I?

NARRATOR/EMCEE. You were tellin' us about how you're a turtle.

HAROLD. Right. I might be. I don't know. And that's what the song is about.
Am I a turtle?
Am I heading for the highway instead of the sea?

(He glances across the crowd.)

I hope you like it.

[MUSIC #2: "CIRCLES IN THE SAND"]

I JUST DON'T KNOW WHAT TO DO
MAYBE I'M A TURTLE TOO
IS THE HIGHWAY MY WAY OR DO I WANT SEA OF BLUE
  – OOO –
MAYBE I'M A TURTLE TOO

YEAH I DON'T KNOW WHAT TO DO
IF THE HIGHWAY I PURSUE
I COULD BE SO FREE ON A FREEWAY OR AVENUE-OOO
OR HIT BY A BMW

TOSSED AND LOST, ADRIFT AND STUCK
DAZED AND FAZED AND OUT OF LUCK
SOMEONE LEND A HELPIN' HAND
SPINNIN' CIRCLES IN THE SAND

(The band kicks in, to **HAROLD**'s *amazement. He gains confidence as he continues to sing.)*

HELP ME OUT, I'M BEGGIN' YOU
SHOULD I CHOOSE THAT SEA OF BLUE?
MAYBE THE FOAM'S LIKE HOME AND THERE'S ALWAYS AN
  OCEAN VIEW – OOO
BUT SHARKS MIGHT MAKE ME TURTLE STEW

SO I SING
LA DA DA DA DA DA DA DA
LA DA DA DA DA DA DA DA

(inviting the audience) Everybody, sing with me!

HAROLD & BAND.

LA DA DA DA DA DA DA DA

HAROLD. *(to audience)* It's easy there are no words!

HAROLD, BAND, AUDIENCE.

LA DA DA DA DA DA DA DA
LA DA DA DA DA DA DA DA

HAROLD, *(to audience)* One more time!

HAROLD, BAND, AUDIENCE.

LA DA DA DA DA DA DA DA

HAROLD,

> TOSSED AND LOST, ADRIFT AND STUCK
> DAZED AND FAZED AND OUT OF LUCK
> IS IT SEA OR IS IT LAND?
> SPINNING CIRCLES IN THE SAND?

> TOSSED AND LOST, ADRIFT AND STUCK
> DAZED AND FAZED AND OUT OF LUCK
> HOW MUCH LONGER CAN I STAND
> SPINNIN' CIRCLES IN THE SAND.

> *(shouting to the band)* One, two, three!

> WHAT DO I DOOOOOOO?
> WHAT DO I DOOOOOOO?
> WHAT DO I DOOOOOOO?
> WHAT DO I DOOOOOOO?

> *(**HAROLD** bows and walks toward the audience.)*

NARRATOR. Of course, in rushing forward so fast, I've skipped over nearly half the story.

> *(**HAROLD** reluctantly halts.)*

And so now instead of going five months forward from:

> *(**MR. MCCLAM** enters.)*

MR. MCCLAM. *(hand on heart)* Cecily...

NARRATOR. And:

HAROLD. *(holding up the guitar)* A guitar?

NARRATOR. We'll go five months back.

> *(**HAROLD** and **MR. MCCLAM** exit.)*

> *[MUSIC #2A: "UNDER SOUTH DAKOTA"]*

Back to the first day of summer, the longest day of the year, which seems even longer if you're stuck in Hill City, South Dakota.

> *(The space transforms into South Dakota. A small house with a window appears, as well as a big tree.)*

Scene 2.
Daphne

(**DAPHNE** *enters with a suitcase.*)

NARRATOR. Ever since Daphne was a little girl she dreamed of being –

DAPHNE. A Broadway star!

NARRATOR. Her main setback was that she was born in Hill City, South Dakota.

A town with a population of less than one thousand.

And so it came as no surprise when one day she told her mother:

DAPHNE. I'm moving to New York City!

NARRATOR/MOTHER. Well, you've been the star of every Hill City Community Theater production. I reckon you're ready for Broadway.

DAPHNE. Can I take the Chrysler?

NARRATOR/MOTHER. The Imperial? That was your father's car. God rest his soul. I still remember the day he bought it.

I wanted black but he insisted on –

NARRATOR/MOTHER & DAPHNE. Seafoam green.

DAPHNE. C'mon, please?

NARRATOR/MOTHER. You can take the car to New York as long as you take your sister with you.

DAPHNE. Of course! I was already planning on it.

[MUSIC #2B: "UNDER PANCAKE HOUSE"]

NARRATOR. Daphne's older sister, Miriam, had spent the last ten years working as a waitress at the Hill City Pancake House.

(**MIRIAM** *enters with a coffee pot. She serves unseen customers.*)

MIRIAM. Refill?

Great!

DAPHNE. Miriam, I'm going to New York! And you're coming with me!

MIRIAM. Why?

DAPHNE. Because. Do you want to live in this house for the rest of your life?

MIRIAM. Yes.

NARRATOR/MOTHER. *(blurts out)* NO!

DAPHNE. Come on, Miriam, you know you love a good adventure.

MIRIAM. You just want someone to cook you dinner.

DAPHNE. That's not all. You're also great at giving pep talks.

MIRIAM. Well... I *have* always wanted to see an ocean.

(*DAPHNE hugs MIRIAM.*)

DAPHNE. *YAY!!* You can navigate. *(handing her a stack of maps)* Maps.
(*taking her arm)* We're leaving immediately!

MIRIAM. *(pulling away, overwhelmed)* Wait!
(quietly) I need the night to pack.

DAPHNE. *Fine...*

NARRATOR. The next morning the girls say goodbye to their mother.

(*DAPHNE re-enters and takes a ring off her finger.*)

DAPHNE. I've got a goodbye present for you, Mom.

NARRATOR/MOTHER. Your lucky ring? Won't you need it in The Big Apple?

DAPHNE. *(giving her the ring)* No, I want you to have it.

NARRATOR/MOTHER. *(to herself)* Well, that's strange.

DAPHNE. *(to MIRIAM)* There can we go now?

MIRIAM. Okay.

(*The girls hug their mother goodbye.*)

DAPHNE. We'll miss you, Mom.

MIRIAM. Don't get too lonely.

NARRATOR/MOTHER. Oh, I'll be fine...

NARRATOR. And with that, they were off!

[MUSIC #3: "DAPHNE DREAMS"]

(The girls get in the Chrysler. MIRIAM *opens up a map, confused.)*

DAPHNE. Here we go!

MIRIAM. Goodbye, South Dakota!

NARRATOR. But as soon as they crossed the state line…

DAPHNE. *(slamming on the brakes)* AH! I can't do this! What was I thinking? I'll never make it in New York.

MIRIAM. Of course you will. You're a star.

DAPHNE. In Hill City.

MIRIAM. You're a star.

DAPHNE. I'm all talk!

MIRIAM. You're a star!

DAPHNE. See? You're so good at pep talks!

MIRIAM. Now I want to hear you say it.

DAPHNE.

> I'M A MOONBEAM IN A FOG
> I'M A STREAM ABOUT TO FLOW
> THEY SAY NEW YORK'S DOG-EAT-DOG
> BUT I'M A SECRET THEY DON'T KNOW
> OH, SISTER, LOOK AT ME!
> HEADING EAST TO NYC!

MIRIAM. *(turning the map around to the correct direction)* Oh!

DAPHNE.

> ONCE YOU KNOW THAT YOU'RE A BIRD WHO'LL SOAR
> YOU'RE SURE TO GET REAL FAR

MIRIAM. And what are you?

DAPHNE.

> I'M A STAR!!!

NARRATOR. Once in New York, Daphne gets a job selling coats and shoes.

*(*DAPHNE *arranges coats on a rack as she sings.)*

DAPHNE.

> I'M A RIBBON ON A SPOOL
> I'M A PRETZEL WHEN IT'S DOUGH
> I'M A TREND BEFORE IT'S COOL
> A SECRET THAT THEY STILL DON'T KNOW

> (**HAROLD** *enters and approaches her.*)

HAROLD. Hi, sorry to bother you.

DAPHNE.

> OH STRANGER LOOK AT ME

HAROLD. I'm looking for a black wool coat.

DAPHNE.

> I CAN BELT ABOVE HIGH C

HAROLD. Wow.

> (**DAPHNE** *puts a coat on* **HAROLD**.)

DAPHNE.

> IF YOU WANT MY VOTE THIS TYPE OF COAT
> WAS WORN BY FDR

> (*examining the price tag*) A new deal!

HAROLD. It's perfect, how did you – ?

DAPHNE.

> I'M A STAR

> (**HAROLD** *exits as* **MIRIAM** *enters.*)

NARRATOR. At home, in the small apartment she shares with Miriam, Daphne amasses a library of plays. She reads them at night and sighs.

DAPHNE. Oh Miriam – do you even know how many wonderful roles there are for women in the theater? I want to play all of them! If only I could get someone else to believe in me besides me.

MIRIAM. And me.

DAPHNE. And you.

NARRATOR. One night Miriam looks out the window and asks:

MIRIAM. Where's the Chrysler?

DAPHNE. I sold it.

(sheepishly) I needed the money for headshots.

MIRIAM. Unbelievable!

*(**MIRIAM** storms off.)*

NARRATOR. Armed with her headshots, Daphne goes to auditions with a renewed sense of confidence.

*(Time passes as **DAPHNE** waits in line at various auditions. She tries to give her headshot to **NARRATOR**/ **PRODUCER** but each time he hands it back.)*

DAPHNE.

I'M A FACE YOU CAN'T IGNORE

NARRATOR/PRODUCER. You're not what we're looking for!

DAPHNE.

I'M A RACECAR GAINING SPEED

NARRATOR/PRODUCER. You're just not what we need!

DAPHNE. Fine.

(to herself)

GOD I'M TIRED OF THESE LINES
BUT IT TAKES PATIENCE TO SUCCEED

NARRATOR. And then, finally –

DAPHNE. *(deep breath)* Finally!

*(**NARRATOR** hands **DAPHNE** a script as **JOEY** enters.)*

JOEY. Hi, I'm Joey Storms, the playwright.

DAPHNE. *(holding out headshot)* Here's my headshot.

*(**JOEY** takes the headshot as **PRODUCER** shakes his head.)*

NARRATOR/PRODUCER. Nope! Next!

DAPHNE.

BUT I'VE BEEN PRACTICING ALL NIGHT

NARRATOR/PRODUCER.

SORRY TOOTS BUT YOU AIN'T RIGHT

JOEY. *(to **NARRATOR**)* Really? We should at least let her –

NARRATOR/PRODUCER.

JOEY USE YOUR EYES HER THUNDER THIGHS

ARE WIDER THAN MY CAR

DAPHNE. Hey! I can hear you! GO TO HELL!

(to **JOEY**) Oh, and you should know your script stinks worse than *GARBAGE!*

(**DAPHNE** *throws the script down as she runs off.*)

JOEY. Wait!

NARRATOR/PRODUCER. Let her go. She's a nobody!

JOEY. (*transfixed*) She's a star...

(**JOEY** *exits.*)

NARRATOR. Back at the store, Daphne's boss implements a new rule:

(as **BOSS**) No more singing at work. This ain't Radio City.

DAPHNE. I'm aware.

NARRATOR/BOSS. You out-of-work actors make lousy salespeople.

DAPHNE. I am *not* an out-of-work actor.

(*singing*) I'M A –

NARRATOR/BOSS. (*shushing her*) Buh buh buh!

(**DAPHNE** *starts to hum the melody but –*)

Eh eh eh!

(*She tries to whistle the melody but –*)

Tsh tsh tsh!

(**DAPHNE** *looks around, defeated.*)

DAPHNE.

GUESS I'LL TAKE THE PART I CAN'T REFUSE
PLAY "THE NO-NAME GIRL OF COATS AND SHOES"

(*softly, to herself*) No, I can't give up...

ALL THE STARS WHO MADE IT TO THE TOP
ARE THE ONES WHO DIDN'T STOP

(**DAPHNE** *leaves the coat store and walks outside.*)

I WON'T EVER FEEL COMPLETE
READING PLAYS FROM OFF A PAGE

WATCHING, SITTING FROM MY SEAT
I WON'T STOP UNTIL I'M CENTER STAGE

'CAUSE STARS AREN'T ONLY IN THE SKY
OR STUCK INSIDE SOME FIREFLY
YOU CAPTURE IN A JELLY JAR
IT ALL DEPENDS ON WHO YOU ARE
AND WHO AM I?
YEAH, WHO AM I?
I'M A STAR!
I'M A STAR!!
YEAH, I'M A STAR!!!

*(***HAROLD*** enters, applauding.* **DAPHNE** *sees him and bows.)*

Scene 3.
Harold & Daphne

NARRATOR. And it's at this point, on a cold December afternoon, that a path that began in Hill City, South Dakota intersects a path that began in Brooklyn, New York.

HAROLD. Are you a singer?

DAPHNE. Slash actress. Yes. Are you a musician?

HAROLD. Yes. Well, trying.

I want to write a song, but right now all I can get out is:

(**HAROLD** *plays one note over and over.*)

DAPHNE. Oh, was that it?

HAROLD. Yup. Say, you look familiar. Would I have seen you in something?

DAPHNE. Not unless you've been to the Hill City Community Theater.

HAROLD. I haven't. But you –

(**CRABBLE** *enters, fuming.*)

CRABBLE. *(to* **HAROLD***)* Harold! Why are you out here during the lunch rush?! Get back inside!

HAROLD. I'll be there. *(thumbs up)* Don't worry.

CRABBLE. Don't *worry?* I remember the LAST time you told me *(thumbs up)* "Don't worry."

(to **DAPHNE***)* Excuse me miss, can you read that sign?

(**CRABBLE** *points to a sign over the shop.*)

DAPHNE. *(reading)* Sandwiches Snadwiches.

What's a Snadwich?

CRABBLE. That's an *excellent* question. Harold, what is a *snadwich?*

HAROLD. *(reciting)* I was in charge of ordering the sign. That *unprofessional* typo is my fault and it does not reflect the quality of our sandwiches it only reflects the quality of me.

CRABBLE. You owe me two hundred dollars for that sign, Harold! And you're *not* gonna earn it out here, unless you start turning tricks and *nobody* wants to see *that*, so *get back inside!*

(CRABBLE *exits.*)

DAPHNE. I should get back to work too. I work at the Coat and Shoe Store around the corner.

HAROLD. Yes! That's how I know you! You sold me a black wool coat last month for my mother's funeral.

DAPHNE. Oh.

HAROLD. I'm Harold.

DAPHNE. I'm Daphne. How are the sandwiches here?

HAROLD. Not terrible.

DAPHNE. Good enough.

(HAROLD *and* DAPHNE *exit.*)

(*The space transforms into a deli. A counter appears.* CRABBLE *stands behind it, making sandwiches.*)

[MUSIC #3A: "UNDER CRABBLE INTRO"]

NARRATOR. Sandwiches *Sandwiches* is a small midtown deli run by a man who is simply known as Crabble.

(CRABBLE *makes a grumpy sound.*)

The story of Crabble is relatively brief. And it only has one bright spot.

CRABBLE. *(dreamily)* World War Two.

NARRATOR. When he was:

CRABBLE. An air traffic controller!

NARRATOR. Occasionally he'll daydream of long gone days spent on the tarmac, waving his hands at planes, shouting:

CRABBLE. Stop! Go! Yield! Turn!

NARRATOR. Other than that, his existence has consisted of standing behind the same counter of the same deli, repeating the same five words over and over again:

CRABBLE.

MAYONAISSE, MEAT, CHEESE 'N LETTUCE.

NARRATOR. And that's pretty much it.

(The door chimes as **HAROLD** *and* **DAPHNE** *enter.)*

CRABBLE. *(to* **HAROLD***)* I don't pay you to loiter!

HAROLD. I was taking *my break.*

CRABBLE. You wouldn't last a *day* in the air force, Harold! *Not a day!*

HAROLD. Yeah / yeah...

CRABBLE. *Make a sandwich!*

NARRATOR. And so Harold makes Daphne a pastrami on rye. And when he gives it to her their hands brush.

(Their hands brush.)

And they share a look.

(They share a look.)

A look that makes both of their hearts beat slightly faster than usual.

(sound of fast heartbeats)

And makes both of them feel a little bit hopeful.

(sound of swelling hope)

DAPHNE. You're cute. *(handing him a headshot)* My number's on the back of my headshot.

HAROLD. Oh, can I call it?

CRABBLE. *(walking off, disgusted)* Good god...

NARRATOR. They start out as friends because –

*(***DAPHNE** *and* **HAROLD** *are on the phone.)*

DAPHNE. You're not the type of guy I usually go for.

HAROLD. I don't think I could keep up with you.

DAPHNE. Yeah

HAROLD. OK.

(They hang up.)

NARRATOR. Until one day:

(**DAPHNE** *and* **HAROLD** *are on the phone once more.*)

DAPHNE. I'm not doing anything tonight. Just gonna sit at home... *Alone* ... What about you?

HAROLD. I might read a book.

DAPHNE. Harold. If you want something...you need to go for it. Make a move. Take action!

HAROLD. Alright, I *will* read a book!

DAPHNE. I'm not talking about books! *(hangs up)*

HAROLD. *(realizing) OH*...

(hanging up the phone, inspired) Action...

(**HAROLD** *walks to* **DAPHNE**'s *apartment.* **NARRATOR** *hands him flowers.* **HAROLD** *knocks on her door. She answers. He holds up the flowers.*)

Good evening.

DAPHNE. Flowers! What a nice surprise!

HAROLD. I'm full of surprises!

DAPHNE. You are?

HAROLD. No. But something about you is making me want to surprise myself.

For example, it's very surprising to me that I'm doing *(strumming his guitar) THIS:*

[MUSIC #4: "MORE THAN JUST A FRIEND"]

YOU'RE THE KIND OF GIRL I'VE WAITED FOR
I SEE NO USE IN TRYING TO PRETEND
I WOULD RATHER TELL YOU FACE-TO-FACE AS I STAND
    OUTSIDE YOUR DOOR
THAT I THINK I LIKE YOU MORE THAN JUST A FRIEND
THAT I THINK I LIKE YOU MORE THAN JUST A FRIEND

DAPHNE. You wrote a song!

HAROLD. For you!

DAPHNE. You wrote *me* a song!

HAROLD. Yeah.

DAPHNE. I want to sing!

HAROLD. Go for it!

DAPHNE.

YOU'RE THE KIND OF GUY I'VE WAITED FOR
YOU'RE A CUTIE AND YOUR BREATH DOES NOT OFFEND

HAROLD. Thanks.

DAPHNE.

I GET HAPPY WHEN I SEE YOU, IT'S A THING I CAN'T IGNORE
THIS COULD MEAN I LIKE YOU MORE THAN JUST A FRIEND
THIS COULD MEAN I LIKE YOU MORE THAN JUST A FRIEND
(spoken) Want to come inside?

HAROLD. *Yes!*

(They move inside **DAPHNE***'s apartment.)*

AND I DON'T WANT TO SECOND GUESS
THIS FEELING THAT I HAVE

DAPHNE.

AND I DON'T WANT TO SIT AND THINK IT THROUGH

HAROLD & DAPHNE.

IF BOTH OF US ARE FEELING THIS
AND IF WE'RE PRETTY SURE
THEN JUST MAYBE THIS IS SOMETHING WE SHOULD DO

BECAUSE WE CAN'T SEE WHAT THE FUTURE HOLDS
AND WE CAN'T SEE WHAT IS WAITING ROUND THE BEND
MAYBE THIS IS WORTH A GAMBLE, YEAH LET'S SEE HOW
    THIS UNFOLDS
THERE'S A GOOD CHANCE THAT WE COULD BE MORE –

HAROLD.

THIS REALLY ISN'T ALL THAT RISKY

DAPHNE.

WE'LL STILL BE FRIENDS BUT ALSO FRISKY

HAROLD.

SO LET'S MAKE THE CHOICE

DAPHNE.

LET'S LEAP AND SEE

HAROLD & DAPHNE.

I'D LIKE TO LIKE YOU MORE THAN JUST A FRIEND
I'D LIKE TO LIKE YOU MORE THAN JUST A FRIEND
I'D LIKE TO LIKE YOU MORE THAN JUST –

(They kiss.)

NARRATOR. That is the beginning of the romance between Harold and Daphne.

*(**HAROLD** exits as **MIRIAM** enters with a stack of maps.)*

Scene 4.
Miriam

NARRATOR. Now at this point it's necessary to journey back once more to that long summer day in South Dakota on which Daphne declares her intention to leave for New York:

DAPHNE. *(taking* **MIRIAM***'s arm)* Immediately!

MIRIAM. *(pulling away, overwhelmed)* Wait!
(quietly) I need the night to pack.

DAPHNE. *Fine.*

*(***DAPHNE** *exits as* **MIRIAM** *approches* **NARRATOR/ MOTHER**.*)*

MIRIAM. I can't go, Mom.

NARRATOR/MOTHER. That's just jitters talking.

MIRIAM. No, I think it's more than that.
I've always had a bad feeling about leaving Hill City.

NARRATOR/MOTHER. Miriam. I love you. But The Time Has Come.
You need to *move forward.*
Or at least move!
Now study those maps! *(shaking her head)* You've got your father's sense of direction.

MIRIAM. *(proud)* I know.

[MUSIC #5: "STARS, I TRUST"]

(A swing flies in. **MIRIAM** *walks over to it and sits down during the* **NARRATOR***'s speech.)*

NARRATOR. And with that, Miriam goes to the backyard, where she sits on a swing her father once tied to the strongest branch of the tallest tree, and waits for the sun to set.
There are a few things you should know about Miriam. She enjoys being a waitress.

MIRIAM. A lot.

NARRATOR. But her first love is:

MIRIAM. Astronomy!

NARRATOR. Her father taught her the subject. He had hoped to share his love of the cosmos with both of his daughters.

(*DAPHNE enters, looks at the sky, fidgets.*)

But Daphne could never stay still long enough to take things in.

DAPHNE. (*giving up, exploding*) Aaah! So boring!

(*DAPHNE exits.*)

NARRATOR. Miriam, on the other hand, would sit patiently with her dad each night, counting the stars:

MIRIAM. One hundred and forty-one, one hundred and forty-two...

NARRATOR. One day, Miriam's mother told her:

(*as* **MOTHER**) Your father's sick. Don't tell him I told you.

(*as* **NARRATOR**) That night, Miriam's father finds her crying outside.

(*as* **FATHER**) I see your mother told you.

MIRIAM. I'm scared.

NARRATOR/FATHER. Me too. But I think I've got something that'll protect us both from our fears. Wanna see? (*MIRIAM nods and he hands her a book. He turns to a page and points.*) Read that.

MIRIAM. (*reading*) "Nearly all of the elements that make up Earth and its life forms were created inside the heart of a dying star, as it exploded out into the atmosphere." Wow.

NARRATOR/FATHER. See? When that star died, it didn't disappear.

It *reappeared.*

As you.

And me.

And everything.

And that's what happens when we die too.

MIRIAM. Really?

NARRATOR/FATHER. Really really.

MIRIAM. *(amazed)* I'm connected to the stars...

NARRATOR/FATHER. Scientifically speaking, you're connected to *everything.*

And you always will be.

So whenever you're afraid or feeling lost and small, just look up at the sky and trust that there's an invisible family tree connecting it, in all its vastness, directly to you.

MIRIAM. And you.

NARRATOR/FATHER. *(as FATHER)* And me.

(as NARRATOR) And so, on her last night in South Dakota, to calm her so-called jitters, Miriam gazes upward and sings a song her father made up just for her.

MIRIAM.

DEAR TINY DOTS OF TWINKLING LIGHT
IT'S TIME FOR ME TO SAY "GOODNIGHT"
THERE'S SO MUCH MADNESS IN THIS WORLD BUT I FEEL
    SAFE 'CAUSE I'M AWARE
YOU ARE UP THERE

I TRUST STARS
HIGH IN THE SKIES
I TRUST STARS
ANCIENT AND WISE
I'M MADE FROM YOUR DUST
STARS I TRUST

GOODNIGHT, YOU SOUTH DAKOTA STARS
BEYOND THE MOON, THE EARTH AND MARS
LOOK, THERE'S A LION AND ORION, SNAKE AND DRAGON.
COULD THERE BE
STARS THAT MAKE ME?

I TRUST STARS
ARE NEVER GONE
I TRUST STARS

ALWAYS LIVE ON
I'M MADE FROM YOUR DUST
STARS I TRUST

AND SURE SOME FOLKS'LL SAY
THAT ALL OF THIS IS HAY
IT'S JUST A SMOKEY-EYED ROMANTIC NOTION
SO I'LL FEEL OK.
BUT THEY CANNOT DENY
NO MATTER HOW THEY TRY
THAT IT'S A FACT WE'RE ALL CONNECTED
FROM THE GRASS UP TO THE SKY

I HAVE MY MEMORIES
TO DO WITH AS I PLEASE
I KNOW I ALWAYS CAN RECALL THAT
STARRY PERFECT NIGHT IN FALL
WHEN YOU STOOD UNDERNREATH THIS TREE
AND PROMISED YOU WOULD ALWAYS BE...
WITH ME...
I TRUST YOU'RE HERE WITH ME

NARRATOR. Miriam is just beginning to feel better when –

(An owl hoots.)

MIRIAM. An owl? We don't have owls around here.
(to herself) Is that a sign I shouldn't go to New York?
Don't be ridiculous, it's just –

*(The lights in the house go out suddenly. **MIRIAM** 's eyes widen in fear.)*

Well that's ominous.

*(**NARRATOR/MOTHER** calls out from the house.)*

NARRATOR/MOTHER. *Daphne!* How many times do I have to tell you – you can't use your hair dryer while I'm using the toaster oven!

DAPHNE. I'm fixing it, ma! Cool your jets!

NARRATOR/MOTHER. *Language!*

(The lights in the house come on again.)

NARRATOR. The next morning Miriam tells Daphne.

MIRIAM. *(worried)* Last night I got a sign. From the universe. Through your hair dryer. I think there's something dark waiting for me in New York. Dark forces. Darkness. Dark stuff.

DAPHNE. Listen to yourself.

MIRIAM. You believe in this kind of thing too.

Things you can't prove but you can feel.

Like your lucky ring.

DAPHNE. *You* gave me this ring!

MIRIAM. And *you've* never taken it off!

DAPHNE. Because I didn't want *you* to think I didn't like it! I don't *actually* believe it's lucky. Here, watch.

(DAPHNE *takes off her lucky ring.*)

I've got a goodbye present for you, Mom.

NARRATOR/MOTHER. Your lucky ring? Won't you need it in The Big Apple?

DAPHNE. *(giving her the ring)* No, I want you to have it.

NARRATOR/MOTHER. *(to herself)* Well, that's strange.

DAPHNE. *(to* MIRIAM*)* There. Can we go now?

NARRATOR. Despite her reservations, Miriam packs her bags into the seafoam green car and heads to New York City.

(*The space transforms into a New York City street. A fire escape appears.*)

On the first night in their new home, the sisters stand on their fire escape.

Daphne, practicing tongue twisters:

DAPHNE. Unique New York, Unique New York…

NARRATOR. And Miriam counting the stars:

MIRIAM. *(looks up, squinting)* One, two, three…

(*That's it. A beat.*)

THREE SMALL STARS
STILL YOU'LL CONNECT
THREE SMALL STARS

STILL YOU'LL PROTECT
I'M MADE FROM YOUR DUST
STARS I TRUST

NARRATOR/GYPSY. Down below on the street an old voice calls out:

(as **GYPSY***)* "You up there!"

DAPHNE. Me?

NARRATOR/GYPSY. Were you the one singing?

DAPHNE. *(insulted)* No. *I* have training.

NARRATOR/GYPSY. *(to* **MIRIAM***)* YOU!

MIRIAM. Yes?

NARRATOR/GYPSY. Come down here!

MIRIAM. OK!

DAPHNE. Miriam, no!

NARRATOR/GYPSY. Miriam, *yes!*

DAPHNE. You disgusting old kook! Get out of here!

NARRATOR/GYPSY. Very well. We'll meet again sooner or later... *Miriam.*

*(***NARRATOR/GYPSY*** walks off singing...)*

I TRUST STARS
I TRUST STARS
I'M MADE FROM YOUR DUST...

MIRIAM. *(to* **DAPHNE***)* She knows my song!

DAPHNE. She heard you singing it.

MIRIAM. She knew my name!

DAPHNE. Because I said it.

MIRIAM. I'm telling you, Daphne. I have a really bad feeling.

DAPHNE. Just ignore it.

NARRATOR. Miriam is able to ignore it because the next night she opens a newspaper and turns right to:

MIRIAM. *(reading)* An ad for a waitress! At a diner in Brooklyn called The Greasy Spoon Café! It's perfect!

[MUSIC #6: "BREAKFAST ALL DAY"]

NARRATOR/BOSS. And so she drives to the Greasy Spoon Café where the owner asks if she's interested in taking: *(as* **BOSS***)* The Graveyard Shift.

MIRIAM. Um. Can we call it the Twilight Shift?

NARRATOR/BOSS. Sure. When can you start?

MIRIAM. Immediately.

(grabs a coffee pot) Refill? Great!

NARRATOR. Sure enough, Miriam's bad feelings disappear once she begins pouring her energy into pouring coffee.

*(***MIRIAM*** grabs a coffee pot and greets customers.)*

MIRIAM.

WELCOME TO GREASY SPOON CAFÉ

NARRATOR. Greasy Spoon does something Miriam's never heard of:

MIRIAM.

HERE WE SERVE BREAKFAST ALL DAY!
THIS IS THE BEST PLACE IN THE U.S.A.

(spoken) It's like a dream! Picture it:

PANCAKES AT MIDNIGHT
FRENCH TOAST AT DAWN
AND BACON AND EGGS
EATEN WHEN THE SUN IS GONE

(spoken) Refill? Great! Refill? Great!

LET ALL YOUR TROUBLES MELT AWAY
LIKE BUTTER ON BREAKFAST ALL DAY
ALL OF YOUR TASTE BUDS WILL SHOUT HIP (HIP!)
HOORAY!

HERE AT GREASY SPOON CAFÉ!

NARRATOR. Now, while working the graveyard, sorry, *twilight* shift at a tiny diner in the outer reaches of Brooklyn may seem undesirable to some:

*(***DAPHNE*** passes through, regarding **MIRIAM** with disbelief)*

DAPHNE. *(to* **MIRIAM***)* How do you do it?

NARRATOR. Miriam likes it.

She likes driving her father's car to work.

She likes being awake when most people are asleep.

And she likes all of her regular customers.

One in particular quickly becomes her favorite.

(A chime sounds as **MR. MCCLAM** *enters the diner holding his record player.)*

MR. MCCLAM. Two for a booth?

MIRIAM. Sure, Mr. McClam.

[MUSIC #7: "THE RECORD PLAYER"]

Scene 5.
Mr. McClam and His Record Player (Part 1)

NARRATOR. After his wife's death, Mr. McClam tries to reach out to Harold so that they can mourn together the loss of:

(**MR. MCCLAM** *puts his hand on his heart.*)

MR. MCCLAM. Cecily.

NARRATOR. The more Mr. McClam listens to:

MR. MCCLAM. *La Traviata.*

NARRATOR. The more he needs to share the story:

MR. MCCLAM. The war was over, I was living with my folks –

NARRATOR. But when Mr. McClam calls Harold at home:

MR. MCCLAM. *(into phone)* Harold. It's your father.

HAROLD. *(into phone)* Sorry. Gotta go to work.

NARRATOR. And when Mr. McClam calls him at work:

CRABBLE. *(holding up phone)* Harold! It's your father!

HAROLD. *(running off)* Sorry. Gotta go home.

NARRATOR. And so instead of connecting with Harold, Mr. McClam connects with:

MR. MCCLAM. *La Traviata.*

NARRATOR. And after a week of sitting at home, he decides to leave his house. Only as the door swings open and the sun and wind hit his face, he realizes that he cannot step outside alone. So he takes a friend:

(**MR. MCCLAM** *tucks his record player under his arm.*)

They go together to the movies:

MR. MCCLAM. Two for the matinee?

NARRATOR. They go together to the zoo:

MR. MCCLAM. Two for the monkeys?

NARRATOR. And they go together to the diner:

MR. MCCLAM. Two for a booth?

MIRIAM. Sure, Mr. McClam. Welcome back. So sorry to hear about your wife.

MR. MCCLAM. Thank you.

MIRIAM. How are you holding up?

MR. MCCLAM. OK.

MIRIAM. And your son?

MR. MCCLAM. Harold?

Who knows?

He isn't so good with communication.

But on the bright side, I dug up this old record of *La Traviata.*

A gift from my wife on our first wedding anniversary.

She gave it to me because, well, it's a funny story, actually...

The war was over, I was living with my folks and –

NARRATOR/BOSS. *TEENAGERS!!! MIRIAM! MAYDAY!*

MIRIAM. *(to* **MR. MCCLAM***)* Sorry gotta go!

*(***MIRIAM*** rushes off as* **MR. MCCLAM** *waves.)*

MR. MCCLAM. OK. Goodnight.

NARRATOR. As a stampede of high school kids overtakes the diner, Mr. McClam heads home, where he can be alone with:

MR. MCCLAM.

LIBIAMO, LIBIAMO NE'LIETI CALICI

CHE LA BELLEZZA INFIORA

NARRATOR. And that's how he gets by. For a while.

Drowning out his sadness with a song.

While across the river, Harold drowns out his sadness with –

(The final chord of "More Than Just a Friend" plays as **HAROLD** *and* **DAPHNE** *appear, kissing.)*

Scene 6.
Joey

NARRATOR. And now we'll travel forward one month to New Year's Day, 1965 on which Daphne is stuck working the big holiday sale at her store –

(The space transforms into the coat store. A coat rack appears. DAPHNE *sorts through an avalance of coats, frustrated.)*

DAPHNE. *(cursing the customers who did this)* Animals!

NARRATOR. When:

*(*JOEY *pops up from between the coats, overjoyed.)*

JOEY. Go to hell!

DAPHNE. Excuse me?

JOEY. *(holding up her headshot)* Daphne!
Joey Storms – playwright. You auditioned for me last month? Come on, surely you remember – you said my script was garbage?

DAPHNE. I said it was *worse* than garbage.

JOEY. You *do* remember!

DAPHNE. What I *remember* are your producer's *choice* words about my thighs.

JOEY. I fired that jerk. I'm self-producing now. A new show. You were right about the other one. It was rotten. It was gutless. It was –

DAPHNE. *(rapid fire)* Derivative. Amateurish. Offensive.

JOEY. Yes! It was all those things! I always suspected it was! But no one told me the truth!
I suppose everyone wanted to believe it was brilliant. Because of who I am.
Y'see, it's not easy being Joey Storms.

[MUSIC #8: "WHAT YOU DO TO ME"]

For *decades* the Storms family has taken Broadway by – well, we've been *very* successful…

LIFE HASN'T BEEN A BREEZE
BECAUSE MY FAMILY'S
GENUINE EXPERTISE
YOU CAN'T DEBATE

BUT WHEN I WRITE, IT'S ODD
I FEEL LIKE I'M A FRAUD
BUT FOLKS SAY, "OH MY GOD
YOUR SCRIPT IS GREAT."

SO THEY PRODUCE IT
AND I WATCH
I NEED A NOOSE
BUT GRAB A SCOTCH
IT'S LIKE A *BANG*
RIGHT TO THE CROTCH

My producers banned me from my own shows. Apparently I was "distracting" the audience with my "excessively loud groans of despair." I was in a dark place. I was beginning to think the family talent gene had skipped over me and gone straight to my little brother, *(darkening)* Ned. *(A quick beat as he thinks about how much he hates Ned.)*
BUT THEN YOU CAME ON THAT STAGE
AND YOU WERE FILLED RAGE
AND SAID THAT EVERY PAGE
WAS GARBAGE!

DAPHNE. Worse / than garbage.

JOEY. *Worse than garbage!*
OH I KNEW RIGHT THERE AND THEN
I HAD TO SEE YOU AGAIN
BECAUSE MY WHEELS BEGAN TO TURN!
WHICH MADE MY GEARS BEGIN TO CHURN!
WHICH MADE MY BRAIN BEGIN TO BURN!

OH IT'S WHAT YOU DO TO ME
IT'S WHAT YOU DO TO ME
IT'S WHAT YOU DO TO ME
DAPHNE!

DAPHNE. That's nice. Now, if you'll excuse me, I need to get back / to work –

JOEY.

> THERE IS A FIREPLACE
> THAT LIVES INSIDE MY FACE
> IT IS A SACRED SPACE
> WHERE NEW THOUGHTS HATCH
>
> I HAD THE LOGS OF WOOD
> LIKE ANY FIRE SHOULD
> BUT WOOD'S NOT ANY GOOD
> WITHOUT A MATCH!
>
> *(to* **DAPHNE***) You're the match!*
>
> OH YOU INSPIRE
> UP A FIRE
> BURNING HOTTER
> BURNING HIGHER
>
> YOU'RE THE GIRL NEXT DOOR BUT UNIQUE!
> YOU'VE GOT PASSION, PEP AND MYSTIQUE!
> AND I HAVE NOT SLEPT FOR A WEEK
>
> 'CAUSE OF WHAT YOU DO TO ME
> IT'S WHAT YOU DO TO ME
> IT'S WHAT YOU DO TO ME
> DAPHNE!

> You're my muse.

DAPHNE. *(curious)* I am?

JOEY. Yes. And if you hear me out I'll buy the priciest coat you have.

DAPHNE. That's the woman's fur.

JOEY. I'll take it! So I've written a new show. *For you.* It's about the human condition. It's called *The Human Condition*. It's experimental but also accessible. It's funny and it's sad and it's grotesque and it's lovely and it has lots of music and lots of silence and – I know, I *know,* it sounds crazy but it *works!* Or it will work, if… you'll be my leading lady.

Here, read one page of the script –

(**DAPHNE** *takes the script.* **JOEY** *paces, nervously.*)

JOEY.

IT'S JUST A FIRST DRAFT...
AND I HATE THAT LINE...
OH NO, SHE JUST LAUGHED
BUT MAYBE THAT'S FINE(?)
AND I WON'T GET MAD
TELL THE TRUTH IF YOU WOULD
OH – YOU THINK THAT IT'S BAD?

DAPHNE. *(stunned)* I think that it's good.

JOEY. *(even more stunned)* Really?

DAPHNE. Yes! It's... It's...

JOEY.

IT'S WHAT YOU DO TO ME!

DAPHNE.

YOU'VE GOT YOURSELF A MUSE!

(**JOEY** *starts to put on the woman's fur coat.*)

JOEY.

OH IT'S WHAT YOU DO TO ME!

DAPHNE.

OH FINALLY – GOOD NEWS!

JOEY.

IT'S WHAT YOU DO TO ME
IT'S WHAT YOU DO TO ME
IT'S WHAT YOU –

DAPHNE.

I!

JOEY

DO TO ME –

DAPHNE.

YOU!

JOEY.

IT'S WHAT YOU DO TO ME!

(**JOEY** *grabs his bag and starts to take* **DAPHNE**'*s hand.*)

JOEY. Rehearsal starts immediately! Let's go!

DAPHNE. I can't rehearse until after work.

JOEY. Oh, that won't do – I need you full-time. Whatever you're making here I'll match it plus a dollar! See you in an hour!

(turning back, sincere) I love this coat.

*(**JOEY** exits.)*

NARRATOR. And so shortly after informing her boss:

DAPHNE. I quit!

NARRATOR. *(as* **BOSS***)* NO!

(as **NARRATOR***)* Daphne rushes over to Sandwiches Sandwiches:

*(**DAPHNE** enters Sandwiches Sandwiches, catching a flustered **HAROLD** off guard.)*

HAROLD. Daphne! Your lunch break isn't for another hour!

DAPHNE. I know! I –

HAROLD. I just, I want to ask you something important. And I thought I had a few more minutes to practice.

DAPHNE. Practice what?

HAROLD. Well, ok. So to start, I know my New Year's resolution. In 1965 I will be a Man of Action. I had a vision: I was driving clear across the country. And you were sitting next to me. And it made me so happy. And I thought, I wonder if Daphne would want that too?

DAPHNE. I would.

HAROLD. You would?

DAPHNE. Yes, but it'll have to wait because *I just got cast as the lead in a musical!!!*

HAROLD. The lead?!

DAPHNE. The lead!

HAROLD. That's fantastic!

*(**DAPHNE** jumps into his arms as **CRABBLE** enters.)*

CRABBLE. Stop touching each other!

(The phone rings and **CRABBLE** *grumbles as he answers it.)* Yeah?

*(***CRABBLE*** wanders away, talking on the phone.)*

DAPHNE. Rehearsals start immediately!

HAROLD. What about your job?

DAPHNE. I quit! Joey's going to pay so he can have me *full-time!*

HAROLD. Who's Joey?

DAPHNE. The playwright. And also the director. And also the producer.

*(***CRABBLE*** slams down the phone, triumphant.)*

CRABBLE. Yes! Harold! You can kiss your snadwiches goodbye! A new sign is being delivered this afternoon. All you gotta do is sign your name and accept the delivery.

HAROLD. *(thumbs up)* Don't worry.

*(***CRABBLE*** growls at Harold then resumes his sandwich-making.)*

DAPHNE. OK, well I need to get to *rehearsal!*

*(***DAPHNE*** goes to leave, **HAROLD** stops her.)*

HAROLD. Wait!

Uh…I made you lunch.

*(***HAROLD*** gives her a sandwich.)*

DAPHNE. This day couldn't get any better.

*(***DAPHNE*** goes to leave.)*

HAROLD. Wait!

Maybe it can. Uh, cover your eyes.

*(***DAPHNE*** covers her eyes.)*

OK now, count to ten.

DAPHNE. OK…

*(As she counts, **HAROLD** quietly begs **CRABBLE** to let him have this one moment. Then he gets his guitar and some flowers and kneels down in front of **DAPHNE**.)*

One, two, three, four, five, six, seven, eight, nine, ten.

*(**DAPHNE** uncovers her eyes as **HAROLD** strums a chord.)*

[MUSIC #8A: "MORE THAN JUST A FRIEND (REPRISE)"]

HAROLD. *(clearing his throat)* Daphne.
WHO CAN SAY WHAT FUTURE LIES AHEAD
ALL I KNOW IS THAT I WANT YOU IN MY LIFE
AND YOU KNOW YOU WON'T GO HUNGRY 'CAUSE I'LL
     BRING HOME THE BREAD

CRABBLE. Only what hit the floor.

HAROLD.
DO YOU THINK YOU'D MAYBE WANT TO BE MY –

DAPHNE. Yes!

HAROLD. Wait, really?!

*(**DAPHNE** kisses **HAROLD**. **CRABBLE** sheds a single tear in spite of himself and exits.)*

DAPHNE. I have to tell my mother!

HAROLD. I have to tell my father.

DAPHNE. And my sister!

HAROLD. Oh riiiight, your "sister."

DAPHNE. She's real! We just –

DAPHNE & HAROLD. Have opposite schedules.

DAPHNE. That's it. You two are meeting tonight.
I'm calling her right now.

HAROLD. Oooh, I can't wait to meet your *(spooky voice)* Ghost Sister.

DAPHNE. She's not a ghost!

NARRATOR. Daphne's right, Miriam is not a ghost.
But for the past few weeks she's felt like one.

*(**MIRIAM** appears looking exhausted.)*

Scene 7.
The Prophecy

NARRATOR. There are no trains or buses that go anywhere near Greasy Spoon Café. So you can imagine Miriam's horror when she looks out the window one night and asks:

MIRIAM. Where's the Chrysler?

DAPHNE. I sold it.

(sheepish) I needed the money for headshots.

MIRIAM. Unbelievable!

NARRATOR. After that, Miriam is forced into the kind of commute that drives many people out of the city that never sleeps. A train to another train to a bus to a fifteen block walk.

And soon what was once –

MIRIAM. Refill?

Great!

NARRATOR. Turns into –

MIRIAM. *(zombified)* Refill...great...

NARRATOR. Until New Year's Day.

The very same day that:

*(****JOEY*** appears holding **DAPHNE**'s headshot.)*

JOEY. Daphne!

DAPHNE. Yes!

NARRATOR. And only a short while after:

*(****HAROLD*** kneels down and strums his guitar.)*

HAROLD. *(clears his throat)* Daphne.

DAPHNE. Yes!

NARRATOR. Miriam's exhausting commute gets the better of her and somewhere in the middle of her fifteen block walk, her thoughts stray and her feet follow suit until –

*(****MIRIAM*** looks up, alarmed.)*

MIRIAM. Where am I?

NARRATOR. She picks a direction and walks.

   [MUSIC #8B: "THE MAP"]

NARRATOR. *(cont.)* And after a few minutes, she sees it: gleaming in the moonlight like a seafoam green mirage.

MIRIAM. The Chrysler!

NARRATOR. Miriam walks towards the car that first belonged to her father and then her mother and then her and discovers that it now belongs to –

   (**NARRATOR** *becomes the* **GYPSY**.)

MIRIAM. YOU!

NARRATOR/GYPSY. Me!
   YOU!
   Ah-ha!
   I told you we'd meet again sooner or later, *Miriam*...

MIRIAM. Oh...

NARRATOR/GYPSY. You're lost. I'll draw you a map. Step into my parlor.

   (**MIRIAM** *follows the* **GYPSY**.)

MIRIAM. Y'know, I can just ask someone else for / directions.

NARRATOR/GYPSY. Shh! Nonsense!

MIRIAM. I don't really have time for –

NARRATOR/GYPSY. Yes, you do.

MIRIAM. I just have somewhere else to be –

NARRATOR/GYPSY. No, you don't.

   (*The space transforms into the* **GYPSY**'s *parlor. A small table with a crystal ball appears.*)

MIRIAM. *(looking around)* I don't know why I'm here.

NARRATOR/GYPSY. *None of us* do.
   Now. Have a seat.

MIRIAM. *(sitting)* You said you had a map?

GYPSY. Yes. A map of your *destiny*.
Would you like to see it?

MIRIAM. I guess.

NARRATOR/GYPSY. Great. Two dollars.

(**MIRIAM** *hands over the money.*)

Now I just have to wait until I get in the zone, which can take up to like twenty min –

(*The crystal ball lights up. A loud crash on the piano.*)

Aahhh! Oh!
The ball is glowing!

MIRIAM. Isn't that what it's supposed to do?

NARRATOR/GYPSY. (*shaken*) Yes, yes…of course…
(*looking inside the ball, muttering to herself*) Oh…oh now that's just crazy…

MIRIAM. What is it?

NARRATOR/GYPSY. I'm seeing things!!!

(*Piano music corresponds with the mood of the ball. High tinkling notes for good news. Low rumbling notes for bad news.*)

The *good news* is that you are about to meet your true love!

MIRIAM. I am?!

NARRATOR/GYPSY. Yes. And he has music inside of him. Music that will fit perfectly together with your music – like two puzzle pieces!

MIRIAM. Puzzle pieces?

NARRATOR/GYPSY. Yes, *puzzle pieces!* You are destined to be with each other! You will feel it first in your heart. *And then in your bones.* And once you meet, your passionate love affair will begin!

MIRIAM. That sounds great!

NARRATOR/GYPSY. Yes, except the *bad news* is that this man will be completely off limits.

MIRIAM. Oh.

NARRATOR/GYPSY. But then the *good news* is that this love affair will bring you rapturous joy!

MIRIAM. Oh!

NARRATOR/GYPSY. But then the *bad news* is that this love affair will bring you torturous guilt!

MIRIAM. Oh.

NARRATOR/GYPSY. But then the *good news* is that you're going to meet this man – your soulmate – *tonight!*

MIRIAM. Oh!

NARRATOR/GYPSY. But then the *bad news* is that you're wearing that.

    *(***NARRATOR/GYPSY*** laughs)*

MIRIAM. So, is there – ?

    [MUSIC #9: "THE PROPHECY"]

GYPSY. *(sensing something)* Shh! Wait!

MIRIAM. What? What is – ?

NARRATOR/GYPSY. Shut up! I need to concentrate!

    I'VE NEVER FELT A NIGHT AS STRONG AS THIS BEFORE
    THE AIR IS HUMMING AN ELECTRIC BUZZ
    I HAD A PREMONITION YOU'D COME THROUGH MY DOOR
    DO YOU KNOW WHY?

MIRIAM.
    WHY I DON'T KNOW!

NARRATOR/GYPSY.
    BECAUSE!

    THE MOON IS FULL OUTSIDE AND WHEN THE MOON IS
        FULL
    YOU KNOW THAT SHIT IS GONNA HIT THE FAN
    NOW CONCENTRATE AND FOCUS
    ALL YOUR ENERGY
    AS I REVEAL YOUR FATED PLAN

    (spoken) I'm seeing a map!

MIRIAM. A map to what?

NARRATOR/GYPSY. Let's find out!

> YOU'LL LEAVE MY PARLOR, CLOSE YOUR EYES AND SPIN SPIN
> SPIN!
> THEN RUN RUN RUN WITH ALL YOUR MIGHT
> THEN STOP! AND LISTEN TO A VOICE FROM DEEP WITHIN
> YOU'LL KNOW WHICH ROAD IS RIGHT

MIRIAM. These instructions are kind of vague.

NARRATOR/GYPSY.

> THE ROAD WILL FORK
> AND YOU WON'T KNOW WHAT TO DO
> BUT DON'T BE SCARED YOU DON'T HAVE FAR TO GO
> JUST LOOK ABOVE AND YOU'LL SEE A CLEAR DIRECTION

MIRIAM. What?

NARRATOR.

> I DON'T KNOW BUT SOMEHOW YOU'LL KNOW

> *(spoken)* And this thing above you will draw a path
> directly to *your soulmate!*

MIRIAM. How can I be sure it's really him?

NARRATOR/GYPSY. *(annoyed)* I'll ask the ball...

> NOW LISTEN TO ME CAREFULLY
> AND I WILL TELL YOU WHAT I SEE
> THERE ARE THREE
> THERE ARE THREE SIGNS THAT I SEE
> NOW LISTEN CLOSELY TO THE WORDS I SAY
> THERE ARE THREE
> THERE ARE THREE SIGNS THAT I SEE
> QUICK PAY ATTENTION, THEY MIGHT FADE AWAY

> *(spoken)* The first sign comes in the form of...a question!
> WHAT DOES IT LOOK LIKE WHEN TIME STOPS?

MIRIAM.

> WHAT DOES IT LOOK LIKE WHEN TIME STOPS?

NARRATOR/GYPSY.

> I DON'T KNOW
> BUT SOMEHOW YOU'LL KNOW.

> *(spoken)* The second comes in the form of...numbers!

> FIVE, TWO, SEVEN

MIRIAM.

> FIVE, TWO, SEVEN

NARRATOR/GYPSY.

> FIVE, TWO, SEVEN

MIRIAM.

> FIVE, TWO, SEVEN

CHORUS. *(echoing)*

> FIVE, TWO, SEVEN

MIRIAM. What do they mean?

NARRATOR/GYPSY.

> I DON'T KNOW
> BUT SOMEHOW YOU'LL KNOW.
>
> *(spoken)* And now the third sign...oh, I'm not seeing it!
> I'm hearing it!
>
> I'M TUNING IN TO NUMBER THREE
> THE MOST IMPORTANT IN THIS PROPHECY:
> IT IS THE WHISPER OF A MELODY
> LA DA DA DA DA DA DA DA
> LA DA DA DA DA DA DA DA
>
> *(**NARRATOR/GYPSY** takes **MIRIAM**'s hand. A transfer of energy.)*

NARRATOR/GYPSY & MIRIAM.

> LA DA DA DA DA DA DA DA
> LA DA DA DA DA DA DA DA
> LA DA DA DA DA DA DA DA
> LA DA DA DA DA DA DA DA

MIRIAM. *(exhilerated)* What does that mean?

NARRATOR/GYPSY. *(exasperated)* I don't know!!

> BUT SOMEHOW YOU'LL KNOW

MIRIAM.

> SOMEHOW I'LL KNOW

NARRATOR/GYSPY.

> SOMEHOW YOU'LL KNOW

NARRATOR/GYPSY & MIRIAM.

> SOMEHOW YOU'LL (I'LL) KNOW

MIRIAM. Is that it?

NARRATOR/GYPSY. That's it.

[MUSIC #9A: "THE PROPHECY (REPRISE)"]

(The crystal ball flickers. Music starts.)

Wait, maybe…

(The ball goes dark. Music stops.)

No, that's it.

Goodbye! And Happy New Year!

*(**GYPSY** waits for **MIRIAM** to leave.)*

MIRIAM. OK…

*(**MIRIAM** leaves and looks around, uncertain.)*

Well? Here goes nothing –
I LEAVE THE PARLOR, CLOSE MY EYES AND SPIN SPIN SPIN!
I RUN, I RUN, I RUN, I RUN
I STOP AND LISTEN *(to her stomach)* HEY YOU VOICE FROM
    DEEP WITHIN
TELL ME IS THIS ROAD THE ONE?

(spoken) I guess.

*(**MIRIAM** tentatively walks…)*

Walking.
Walking.
Walking.

(stops, amazed)

WOW, IT'S THE FORK!
I CAN'T GO IN BOTH DIRECTIONS
I SHOULD STOP, AND YET I'VE COME THIS FAR
I LOOK ABOVE
I LOOK ABOVE AND I SEE NOTHING

(spotting)

OH BUT WAIT!
IS THAT A SHOOTING STAR?

(Music builds under the following:)

NARRATOR. Miriam follows the shooting star down a street which leads to a dead end. At the end of which is a diner. *Her diner.* She rushes inside and finds...

(Music stops.)

No one.

MIRIAM. Oh.

NARRATOR. And then –

*(**HAROLD** enters holding his guitar.)*

HAROLD. Hi. Can I get a table?

MIRIAM. *(frozen in place)* Uh...I...

NARRATOR/BOSS. *(to **HAROLD**)* Yes. Sit anywhere ya like.
*(to **MIRIAM**)* You're late.

*(**HAROLD** sits down and begins to play his guitar.*
***MIRIAM** tentatively approaches him with coffee.)*

MIRIAM. Coffee?

HAROLD. Uh –

*(**MIRIAM** pours the coffee.)*

Stop! I don't have a cup!

MIRIAM. Oh! Sorry!

HAROLD. It's OK, I'm waiting for someone. Two people actually.

MIRIAM. Oh. Coffee while you wait?

HAROLD. Sure. In a cup, please?

NARRATOR. Miriam goes into the kitchen to collect her thoughts.

MIRIAM. Is the prophecy real?

And if it is, how can I be sure that this man waiting for coffee *in a cup* is the one? *(remembering)* The signs!

*(**MIRIAM** returns to **HAROLD**'s table. She pours a cup of coffee and ventures...)*

Hey, do you know what it looks like when time stops?

HAROLD. Is that a joke?

MIRIAM. No.

HAROLD. Maybe it looks like this?

*(**HAROLD** freezes for a second.)*

MIRIAM. *(skeptical)* Hmmmmm...

*(**MIRIAM** smiles politely and leaves.)*

NARRATOR. After a minute, Miriam returns to try again.

MIRIAM. *(returning)* Refill?

HAROLD. Sure.

MIRIAM. Great. Do the numbers 5, 2, 7 mean anything to you?

HAROLD. I don't think so.

MIRIAM. OK.

NARRATOR. Miriam leaves for a few more minutes and then returns to try again.

MIRIAM. Refill?

HAROLD. Sure.

MIRIAM. Great!

*(**MIRIAM** pours the coffee and "casually" sings to herself [in the tune from "The Prophecy"/"Circles in the Sand"]...)*

LA DA DA DA DA DA DA DA
LA DA DA DA DA DA DA DA

HAROLD. Catchy tune. Did you make it up?

MIRIAM. *(intense)* I don't know. *Did I?*

HAROLD. I don't know... Did you?

MIRIAM. How do you feel about *signs*?

HAROLD. *(growing dark)* I *hate* signs.

MIRIAM. *(disappointed)* Oh.

HAROLD. There's this one at work that's *ruining* my life.

First I was responsible for a typo. And then today a replacement was sent and I was supposed to sign for it but the delivery people came while I was in the bathroom and so now they're transporting it back to the factory in Oklahoma!

MIRIAM. I guess I was talking about something more mystical.

HAROLD. Oh.

MIRIAM. It's possible. I think. Anything's possible. There's so much going on... *(gesturing outwards)* out there. We live on this tiny planet orbiting a star that's one of billions of stars in a galaxy that's one of billions of galaxies.

Sorry, I'm sort of an astronomy nerd.

HAROLD. I'm a nerd too!

MIRIAM. Really, what kind?

HAROLD. Marine biology.

It's a private passion.

Publicly, I make sandwiches. For a living.

MIRIAM. That sounds great!

HAROLD. Yeah, right.

MIRIAM. I'm serious! I bet you're good at it.

HAROLD. Oh, I'm not. But I've embraced mediocrity. It was surprisingly easy.

MIRIAM. How can you say that?

I bet a lot of people look forward to sandwiches made specifically by you.

HAROLD. You think?

MIRIAM. Yeah.

Well, uh, just holler if you need more coffee...

*(**MIRIAM** starts to leave as **HAROLD** plays the guitar and sings to himself.)*

HAROLD.

LA DA DA DA DA DA DA DA

*(**MIRIAM** turns back.)*

Hey, I like that.

I *really* like it, actually.

Can I borrow it?

MIRIAM. Only if you promise to take good care of it.

HAROLD. I will.

(**HAROLD** *starts writing on his napkin.*)

MIRIAM. Do you write songs?

HAROLD. Well, I sort of wrote one. Then I got stuck.
I've been trying to write this other song for a while, but all I have is:

(**HAROLD** *plays the opening chords of "Circles In The Sand."*)

[MUSIC #10: "DINER"]

DOOBIE-DOOBIE-DOOBIE-DOO
DOOBIE-DOOBIE-DOOBIE-DOO

MIRIAM. Wait, sing that again!

HAROLD. An encore?
Unexpected. But, ok...

HAROLD.	**MIRIAM**.
DOOBIE-DOOBIE- DOOBIE-DOO	
	I TRUST STARS
DOOBIE-DOOBIE- DOOBIE-DOO	
	I TRUST STARS
DAH DOO DAH DOO DAH	
DABA DA DOOBIE DABA DA	

HAROLD. Whoa. I just wrote that as I sang that.

(*mind blown*) I *wrote that...*

As I *sang that.*

Okay! And oh! That could go right into your tune!

(*singing*) LA DA DA DA DA DA DA DA

HAROLD & MIRIAM.

LA DA DA DA DA DA DA DA

HAROLD. Yes! What a breakthrough! You're like some kind of magical wizard!

MIRIAM. What other kind of wizard is there?

HAROLD. Hey our songs kind of fit together.

MIRIAM. Like puzzle pieces!

HAROLD. How long have you worked here?

MIRIAM. Since June.

HAROLD. I grew up around the corner. This is my dad's favorite place. He always gets the same thing:

Two eggs sunny side up, one slice of cantaloupe, a slice of white toast, a slice of rye toast –

HAROLD & MIRIAM. Half a grapefruit and a cup of coffee!

MIRIAM. You're Harold!

HAROLD. And you're Miriam.

MIRIAM. How did you –

HAROLD. *It's a sign.*

MIRIAM. Oh my / god.

HAROLD. And it's on your / nametag.

MIRIAM. OK, I have to say something. Tonight I met this psychic gypsy. And she saw a map in her crystal ball and told me it would lead me to my soulmate.

So I followed the map and it led me here.

And she gave me three signs so I'd know when I met the one.

The first, a question: "What does it look like when time stops?"

The second, numbers: 5, 2, 7.

And then the third sign was a melody: *(singing)*

LA DA DA DA DA DA DA DA!

HAROLD. I –

MIRIAM. And I don't know why you think you're in this diner right now. But whatever the reason is, it's not the real reason. Because the real reason you're here is to meet me.

HAROLD. I'm –

MIRIAM. You're my soulmate.

I think.

(HAROLD stares at her. A beat.)

(The door chimes and DAPHNE enters.)

DAPHNE. Sorry I'm late!

Rehearsal went way longer than expected!

Good! You two found each other!

(making introductions) Harold, Miriam. Miriam, Harold.

(to **HAROLD***)* See, told ya she wasn't a ghost!

(to **MIRIAM***)* This is the guy I was telling you about!

HAROLD. *(to* **MIRIAM***)* You're – ?

DAPHNE. *(to* **HAROLD***)* You didn't tell her / did you?

HAROLD. You didn't tell me she *worked* here.

DAPHNE. I thought / I did.

MIRIAM. What's going on?

DAPHNE. Miriam...I got engaged!

> *(She holds up the script.) And* I *also* got cast as the lead in a musical!

> It's like the stars are all aligned for me or something.

> Ah! Miriam! *I'm talking about stars!*

> *(to* **HAROLD***)* She's really into that kind of stuff. Right, Miriam?

MIRIAM. Right.

DAPHNE. *(to* **MIRIAM***)* Now, I know what you're thinking:

> They've only been dating a month! That seems awful fast!

> But sometimes when you meet the right person, you just know, y'know?

> *(to* **HAROLD***)* Right?

HAROLD. Right.

DAPHNE. We picked out a date.

> May 27th.

> *(***HAROLD** *looks at* **MIRIAM***.)*

HAROLD. 5, 2, 7...

DAPHNE. That's another way to say it, yes. Anyway... Will you be my maid of honor?

MIRIAM. Yes! Of course!

> *[MUSIC #11: "SAD BREAKFAST"]*

NARRATOR. Believe it or not this is not the worst part of
Miriam's night.

After Harold and Daphne leave:

DAPHNE. Bye!

HAROLD. Nice meeting you.

(**HAROLD** *and* **DAPHNE** *exit.*)

NARRATOR. Miriam tries to cheer herself up:

MIRIAM. *(sadly)*
I CAN'T FEEL AWFUL
WHILE SERVING A WAFFLE

NARRATOR. But it doesn't work. And when her shift ends at
7 a.m., she begins her long journey home, shoulders
slumped and head down, so that it comes as a real
shock when she walks directly into:

[MUSIC #12: "THE PROPHECY PART 2"]

NARRATOR. *(becoming the* **GYPSY***)* Miriam!

MIRIAM. Oh my god!

NARRATOR/GYPSY. I've been searching for you for hours!

MIRIAM. You have?

NARRATOR/GYPSY. Yes. You're a hard woman to find.

MIRIAM. But I just work down the street. And you're
psychic.

NARRATOR/GYPSY. There was MORE!
After you left! The ball lit up again!
Revealing a second part of the prophecy!
You will have a love affair with your soulmate.
And then you will have…
A Great Fall.

MIRIAM. Huh?

NARRATOR. A Great Fall!

MIRIAM. Do you mean a great fall, like the season? Like,
mmm, smell that air, what a great fall?

NARRATOR/GYPSY. No, that's not what I mean.

I'm afraid you have what's known *in the biz* as a mountain life.

A life whose path climbs up, up, up...and then DOWN.

MIRIAM. No.

NARRATOR/GYPSY. Yes.

MIRIAM. Is there any way to stop this from happening?

NARRATOR/GYPSY. I'll tell you for another dollar.

(**MIRIAM** *gives* **GYPSY** *another dollar.*)

No.

(soft)

A GREAT FALL
A GREAT FALL IS HEADED FOR YOU
I ASSURE YOU, THERE IS NO ESCAPE

(very loud)

A GREAT FALL!
A GREAT FALL!
A GREAT FALL!
A GREAT FALLLLLLLLLLLLLLLLLLLLLLLLLLLLLLL!!!!!!

MIRIAM. So now what am I supposed to do?

NARRATOR/GYPSY. Go! Live your life!

Claim your destiny.

ALL. OF. IT.

MIRIAM. *All of it?*

NARRATOR. Yes all of it. Okay, see you later.

(**NARRATOR/GYPSY** *exits leaving* **MIRIAM** *bewildered.*)

Scene 8.
The Triangle

NARRATOR. Miriam doesn't know quite what to make of the gypsy's predictions but she does know that under no circumstances can she see or talk to Harold ever again.

Unfortunately this becomes difficult when:

(DAPHNE appears and asks MIRIAM:)

DAPHNE. Will you go see Harold and talk to him?

NARRATOR. And why does Daphne make this request? To find out we must take a quick trip through the winter months.

First, there's January when Joey realizes that everything he's written is:

(JOEY enters, waving his script around.)

JOEY. Wrong! All wrong!

NARRATOR. So he goes into a small office for several hours until he emerges with:

JOEY. More scenes!

(JOEY hands DAPHNE a bunch of pages.)

NARRATOR. On her lunch break Daphne goes to Sandwiches Sandwiches and:

(DAPHNE goes to Sandwiches Sandwiches, trailed by JOEY.)

HAROLD. *(to DAPHNE)* Made you lunch!

DAPHNE. Thanks! Harold, this is Joey.

JOEY. *(holds out his hand, not looking up from his script)* Joey Storms.

HAROLD. Harold McClam. *(to DAPHNE)* I'm writing a new song! Wanna hear?

DAPHNE. Yes! Later.

(kissing his cheek) I gotta go to rehearsal! Bye!

JOEY. Bye!

[MUSIC #13: "THE TRIANGLE"]

NARRATOR. And at night:

> (**DAPHNE** *goes home.* **MIRIAM** *sits on a small couch, reading.*)

DAPHNE. *(to* **MIRIAM***)* I don't want to fall behind on the wedding.
Can you hire a florist? I trust you.

MIRIAM. No problem.

NARRATOR. And then there's February when:

> (**JOEY** *hands* **DAPHNE** *a bunch of pages.*)

JOEY. More scenes!

NARRATOR. And:

> (**DAPHNE** *and* **JOEY** *go to Sandwiches Sandwiches where* **HAROLD** *holds out a lunch bag.*)

HAROLD. *(to* **DAPHNE***)* Here's your lunch.

DAPHNE. Great.

JOEY. Hey Henry!

HAROLD. It's Harold. *(to* **DAPHNE***)* My song's gonna be about a sea turtle. Wanna hear?

DAPHNE. Yes! *(kissing his cheek)* But I gotta go. Bye.

JOEY. Bye!

> (**DAPHNE** *goes home to* **MIRIAM**.*)

NARRATOR. And:

DAPHNE. Do you think you can book a church? And pick out a cake flavor? I trust you.

MIRIAM. No problem.

NARRATOR. Which then brings us to March when:

> (**JOEY** *hands* **DAPHNE** *a bunch of pages.*)

JOEY. More!

> (**DAPHNE** *and* **JOEY** *go to Sandwiches Sandwiches where* **HAROLD** *holds out a paper bag.*)

HAROLD. Food.

(**DAPHNE** *is reading new pages and forgets to take the sandwich.*)

JOEY. Herman.

HAROLD. Harold.

DAPHNE. Bye.

JOEY. Bye!

(**DAPHNE** *goes to* **MIRIAM.**)

DAPHNE. Can you book a band?

MIRIAM. What kind?

DAPHNE. I trust you. Oh, actually. Harold will have an opinion about this.

MIRIAM. OK, let me know what he says.

DAPHNE. I don't have time. We're rehearsing around the clock! Will you go see Harold and talk to him?

NARRATOR. And so we land on April 1st.

Exactly three months to the day from:

MIRIAM. You're my soulmate.

I think.

NARRATOR. When:

(*The deli door chimes and* **MIRIAM** *walks in to find* **HAROLD** *behind the counter.*)

MIRIAM. Hi.

HAROLD. Oh!

MIRIAM. Sorry.

HAROLD. No.

MIRIAM. I.

HAROLD. I'm.

MIRIAM. I'm here.

HAROLD. You're here.

MIRIAM. I'm here to ask you: What kind of band do you want to play at your wedding reception?

HAROLD. Uh, I dunno.

MIRIAM. Rock band? String quartet?

HAROLD. Sure.

MIRIAM. Cool.

Wait, / which one?

HAROLD. So hey, I know things are a little weird between us –

MIRIAM. What? No they / aren't.

HAROLD. On New Year's. At Greasy Spoon, I should've –

MIRIAM. I don't even know what you're talking about! / What?

HAROLD. I've been wanting to call you. I thought that we could maybe –

(**CRABBLE** *appears, on the phone.*)

CRABBLE. *MICHIGAN?!?*

What the hell's it doing in Michigan?!

(**CRABBLE** *hangs up.*)

Harold!

That sign should have been hanging above this deli months ago!

But instead, you sent it on some kind of an *odyssey! An ODYSSEY!*

(**CRABBLE** *marches off, furious. After a moment,* **HAROLD** *turns back to* **MIRIAM**.)

HAROLD. I thought about you the other day while I was in the shower.

MIRIAM. *What?*

HAROLD. Because that's where I came up with some lyrics for my song. Wanna hear?

MIRIAM. OK.

HAROLD. Cool! OK, here's what I've got so far:

[MUSIC #14: "CIRCLES IN THE SAND (REPRISE 2)"]

(singing and playing)

TURTLE TURTLE TURTLE OOOH
THERE'S A TURTLE ON MY SHOE –

I'm having a hard time finding the right words. Maybe you could help me – ?

MIRIAM. *(turning)* I have to go.

HAROLD. Wait, do you want a sandwich?

(HAROLD holds out a paper bag with a sandwich.)

Here. A customer forgot it.

MIRIAM. What if they come back?

HAROLD. I want you to have it.

(MIRIAM takes the bag. She looks inside.)

MIRIAM. That's great looking sandwich.
See? I knew you were good at your job.

HAROLD. Maybe it's falling in love.

MIRIAM. What?

HAROLD. What it looks like…when time stops.

MIRIAM. Oh.

HAROLD. Um.

MIRIAM. I –

HAROLD. OK.

MIRIAM. Yeah. I'll see you at your wedding to my sister! Bye!

(MIRIAM rushes out.)

NARRATOR. Immediately upon exiting Sandwiches Sandwiches, Miriam resumes her plan to avoid Harold at all costs but the very next morning:

(MIRIAM's phone rings.)

MIRIAM. Hello?

HAROLD. Miriam?

MIRIAM. *(hanging up)* Ack!

HAROLD. Wait –

NARRATOR. And so that day Harold calls in sick to work:

HAROLD. *(coughing into the phone)* I think it's bronchitis.

CRABBLE. *(hanging up)* Lies!

NARRATOR. And he sits at home and:

(**HAROLD** *plays one note over and over again on his guitar. For a while. At least ten seconds.*)

Until he finally finds the right words:

(**HAROLD** *lights up, inspired.*)

HAROLD.

I JUST DON'T KNOW WHAT TO DO
MAYBE I'M A TURTLE TOO

NARRATOR. And as the morning goes on, his neighbors can hear him singing at the top of his lungs!

HAROLD.

HELP ME OUT I'M BEGGING YOU!!!
SHOULD I CHOOSE THAT SEA OF BLUE??!!!

NARRATOR. And before long Harold realizes that he needs to share his song.

(**HAROLD** *sings while dialing his phone.*)

HAROLD.

LA DA DA DA DA DA DA DA

(**MIRIAM**'s *phone rings.*)

MIRIAM. Hello?

HAROLD. *(into the phone)*

LA DA DA DA DA DA DA DA

MIRIAM. Goodbye.

NARRATOR. And that's when he comes up with his ingenious plan.

HAROLD. Ha!

(**HAROLD** *dials.*)

MIRIAM. Hello?

HAROLD. Miriam?

MIRIAM. Goodb –

HAROLD. I found the perfect band for the wedding!

MIRIAM. OK, give me their phone / number and –

HAROLD. I can't. *These guys don't believe in phones.*

MIRIAM. What?

HAROLD. But they're playing tonight.

NARRATOR. And *that's* how Harold gets Miriam to come to a small, smoky club to listen to his song.

(The space tranforms into a nightclub once more. **MIRIAM** *sits off to the side, watching* **HAROLD**.*)*

HAROLD. *(glances across the crowd at Miriam)* I hope you like it.

NARRATOR. And now we've arrived back at the moment I rushed towards earlier! A crucial crossroads!

HAROLD.

TOSSED AND LOST ADRIFT AND STUCK
DAZED AND FAZED AND OUT OF LUCK
HOW MUCH LONGER CAN I STAND?
SPINNIN' CIRCLES IN THE SAND

(shouting to the band) One, two, three!
WHAT DO I DOOOOOOO?
WHAT DO I DOOOOOOO?
WHAT DO I DOOOOOOO?
WHAT DO I DOOOOOOO?

*(***HAROLD*** *bows and walks toward* **MIRIAM**.*)*

Did you like my song?

MIRIAM. You tricked me.

HAROLD. Yes.

Did you like my song?

MIRIAM. It doesn't matter.

HAROLD. Yes, it does.

MIRIAM. No, it doesn't.

HAROLD. Yes it does. Yes it does.

MIRIAM. No, it really *really* doesn't!

HAROLD. Just tell me if you liked it!

MIRIAM. Yes, I liked it, ok. I loved it. Are you happy? I'm going home.

HAROLD. It's about –

MIRIAM. I know what it's about.

HAROLD. Oh – I wasn't sure if you'd get the metaphor.

MIRIAM. Of course I got it, it was really obvious.

HAROLD. I appreciate your criticism.

MIRIAM. You shouldn't have done this.

HAROLD. Miriam –

MIRIAM. Harold. Don't.

HAROLD. I can't stop thinking about you.

NARRATOR.

　　INSTANTS...

HAROLD. I know you feel the same way I do.

NARRATOR.

　　MOMENTS...

MIRIAM. Well...you're wrong.

NARRATOR.

　　ONE FLICKERING FLAME OF LIGHT
　　MMMM...

　　*(***HAROLD** *and* **MIRIAM** *kiss.)*

　　(Blackout.)

End of Act One

ACT TWO

Scene 1.
The Middle

[MUSIC #15: "PULLED APART"]

(NARRATOR enters.)

NARRATOR. As I said before, our story tonight circles around a triangle.

And like a triangle, it has three parts.

What you've just seen is the first part.

This is the next part.

The second part.

We'll resume our tale moments after a crucial crossroads has been reached!

(HAROLD and MIRIAM enter and kiss. After a beat they break apart.)

HAROLD. Wow.

MIRIAM. Whoa.

NARRATOR/EMCEE. Hey, Turtle Man!

HAROLD. What do we do now?

NARRATOR/EMCEE. Get your crap outta the dressing room!

MIRIAM. I don't know. Sounds like you gotta get your crap outta the dressing room.

NARRATOR/EMCEE. Now!

HAROLD. I heard you! *(to MIRIAM) Okay.* We'll figure this out. Everything's gonna be fine. I'll be back in a flash! Wait right there! Don't move!

(**HAROLD** *runs off as fast as he can.*)

NARRATOR. As Harold runs off, Miriam's mind begins to race:

MIRIAM.

WAIT, STOP – WHAT'S HAPPENING?!
I HAVE NEVER FELT SO HAPPY
I HAVE NEVER FELT SO SICK
HE'LL BE BACK IN JUST A MINUTE
GOTTA MAKE A CHOICE AND QUICK

AN INSTANT, JUST A MOMENT
HE'S WITH DAPHNE, HE'S NOT THE ONE
MY HEART IS BURSTING
IT'S THE BEST
THING – OH GOD – THE WORST THING
I'VE EVER DONE!

IT'S CLOSER THAN BEFORE
A DARK FORCE I CAN'T IGNORE
WHAT DO I DO?
MY HEAD AND HEART
ARE BEING PULLED APART
WHAT DO I DO?
STOP AT THE START
BEFORE I'M PULLED APART?

OH, BUT WHEN I HEAR THAT MELODY
I FEEL ALIVE, I FEEL ELATED, I FEEL FREE!
NO! I HAVE TO STOP THIS
NEED TO DROP THIS NONSENSE
I WON'T BE SO NAÏVE
I KNOW – I HAVE TO LEAVE!

(**MIRIAM** *runs away.*)

NARRATOR. And so when Harold returns less than a minute later.

(**HAROLD** *runs back onstage.*)

HAROLD. *(looking around)* Miriam?
(to himself) Where'd she go?

NARRATOR. While Harold searches the streets for:

HAROLD. *(calling) Miriam!*

    *(**HAROLD** exits.)*

NARRATOR. Miriam goes back to the apartment she shares with:

    *(**MIRIAM** appears in her apartment, frantically packing as **DAPHNE** enters.)*

MIRIAM. Daphne! Oh god! I'm so sorry! For everything!

DAPHNE. What are you talking about?

MIRIAM. I never should have come with you to New York. I knew there was a dark force here.

DAPHNE. Not this again...

MIRIAM. It's creeping closer now. I can actually feel it pulling on me.

DAPHNE. That's your pantyhose. You gotta spring for the good kind, Miriam.

MIRIAM. Look. I can't explain it but I need you to believe me... I *know* that if I stay in New York... I'll...

DAPHNE. You'll what?

MIRIAM. It'll be better for both of us if I leave.

DAPHNE. You're not making any sense!

MIRIAM. Just trust me.

DAPHNE. Why are you doing this?

MIRIAM. I'm sorry!

    *(**MIRIAM** runs off.)*

NARRATOR. And so, instead of continuing down the path with Harold, Miriam chooses a route that takes her half-way across the country to the doorstep of a very surprised woman:

NARRATOR/MOTHER. Miriam?

MIRIAM. Hi Mom! You said I could always come home...

NARRATOR/MOTHER. I did?

NARRATOR. And not long after Miriam makes the trip back
   to South Dakota, both Harold and Daphne realize
   they *can't* make the trip to the altar.

   (**HAROLD** *and* **DAPHNE** *enter.*)

NARRATOR. I'm afraid a chasm of doubt has grown between
   our two young lovers since:

   (**HAROLD** *kneels down to propose and strums his guitar.*)

HAROLD. Daphne.

DAPHNE. Yes!

NARRATOR. Now, when they imagine their marriage vows,
   all either one can hear is:

HAROLD & DAPHNE. For worse
   For poorer
   For weaker
   In sickness
   'Til death.

NARRATOR. Which is why as May 27th draws near:

DAPHNE. I don't have time for anything except rehearsals.

HAROLD. I'm swamped with sandwiches.

DAPHNE. I think we should postpone our wedding.

HAROLD. Me too.

DAPHNE. But we should move in together.

HAROLD. Me too. Wait, what?

DAPHNE. I can't afford my place without Miriam's half of
   the rent.

HAROLD. So Miriam's really gone?
   I thought maybe she was just taking a trip.

DAPHNE. No. She's done with New York.

HAROLD. Done?

DAPHNE. Yeah. So can I move in with you?

HAROLD. Of course.

NARRATOR. And so Daphne moves into Harold's fifth floor
   walk-up apartment. But despite sharing a home, they
   see each other less than before because:

(JOEY *enters, stressed.*)

JOEY. We need longer rehearsals!

HAROLD. Is this show ever going to open?

NARRATOR. Daphne wonders the same thing until finally Joey announces:

JOEY. The Human Condition will open on November 9th!

DAPHNE. Yay!

HAROLD. Yaaay…

    (JOEY *exits.* HAROLD *turns to* DAPHNE.)

Wanna catch a movie?

DAPHNE. I'd love to. But I've got –

DAPHNE & HAROLD. Rehearsal. Bye…

    (DAPHNE *exits*)

NARRATOR. As the weeks go by, Harold finds himself increasingly fixated on –

HAROLD. I never should've gotten my crap outta that dressing room!

I was very clear. I said, "Wait right there! Don't move!"

NARRATOR. Harold tries to contact Miriam to find out:

HAROLD. Why'd she move? Does she hate me?

NARRATOR. But no matter how many times he calls:

    (HAROLD *picks up the phone.*)

HAROLD. Is Miriam there?

NARRATOR. *(as* MOTHER*)* I told you. She's not taking any phone calls from men!

(as NARRATOR*)* Eventually he tries…

HAROLD. *(in a high-pitched voice)* Phone call for Miriam?

NARRATOR/MOTHER. Honey, please! I know the sound of a man pretending to be a woman.

Now I don't know who you are but you need to leave my daughter alone! She's scared enough as it is!

HAROLD. Scared?

NARRATOR/MOTHER. I've said too much! Now stop calling! It's getting creepy!

HAROLD. *(still high-pitched)* My apologies.

*(**HAROLD** hangs up the phone and starts to absentmindedly play his guitar.)*

LA DA DA DA DA DA –

(stopping himself) It's getting creepy...

NARRATOR. Harold stares at his guitar. Hating himself for taking:

HAROLD. Action.

(looking at his guitar) I need to stop.

NARRATOR. And so, he hides his guitar in his closet. And tries to forget about –

HAROLD. Miriam...

NARRATOR. Meanwhile, Miriam is back in South Dakota trying to forget about –

*(**MIRIAM** appears, singing.)*

MIRIAM.

I JUST DON'T KNOW WHAT TO DO
(to herself, annoyed) Stop singing!

NARRATOR. And she'll remain there, trying not to sing, for spring, summer and most of fall until one day, out of the blue –

*(**MIRIAM** is nervously knitting when her phone rings. It startles her and she gasps.)*

MIRIAM.*(answering the phone, tentatively)* Hellooo?

DAPHNE. *(on the phone)* Miriam?

NARRATOR. But I'm rushing ahead again. Back to Harold. As the months go by, Harold's favorite time of day becomes nighttime. Because nighttime means bedtime and bedtime means dreaming and dreaming is the only way he can see:

HAROLD. Miriam...

*(**MIRIAM** floats through.)*

MIRIAM. You're my soulmate... I think...

NARRATOR. And even when he's not in bed, he finds himself daydreaming more and more about –

HAROLD. *(to* **MIRIAM***)* Miriam.

I can't stop thinking about you.

I know you feel the same way I do.

(As **MIRIAM** *exits,* **CRABBLE** *enters.)*

CRABBLE. *I don't!*

Now snap out of it!

NARRATOR. Eventually Harold's longing turns into sadness:

HAROLD. *(to* **CRABBLE***, sadly)* Fine…

NARRATOR. And then sadness turns into frustration:

CRABBLE. Snap out of it and make a sandwich!

[MUSIC #16: "ETERNITY"]

HAROLD. Fine!

NARRATOR. And then, his frustration turns into –

CRABBLE. I said, mmmake a –

HAROLD. *(angry)* I said / *FIIIIINE!!!*

CRABBLE.

SAAAANDWICH!!!!

HAROLD.

MAYONNAISE MEAT CHEESE 'N LETTUCE
MAYONNAISE MEAT CHEESE 'N LETTUCE
MAYONNAISE MEAT CHEESE 'N LETTUCE
MAYONNAISE MEAT CHEESE 'N LETTUCE…
I'M A ROBOT WHO IS PROGRAMMED TO PERFORM A
    ROUTINE
A MACHINE

CRABBLE. Faster!

HAROLD.

INSTEAD OF SPREADING MAYO THERE'S A BETTER USE FOR
    THIS KNIFE:
TAKE MY LIFE!

CRABBLE. McClam!

HAROLD.

OR I THINK THAT WHEN CRABBLE ISN'T LOOKIN'
I SHOULD SINK IT IN BETWEEN HIS SHOULDERS – NOW
    WE'RE COOKIN'!

CRABBLE.

DO YOUR JOB BECAUSE THERE AIN'T ANOTHER FUTURE IN
    SIGHT

HAROLD.

GOD, HE'S RIGHT!
IS THIS MY LIFE NOW?
IS THIS IT?

CRABBLE.

THIS IS HOW IT'S GONNA BE
THIS IS YOUR LIFE NOW

HAROLD.

THIS IS SHIT

CRABBLE.

TILL ETERNITY

CRABBLE & HAROLD.

MAYONNAISE MEAT CHEESE 'N LETTUCE
MAYONNAISE MEAT CHEESE 'N LETTUCE…

CRABBLE.

WHEN YOU'RE YOUNG YOU THINK THAT YOU WILL DO
    WHATEVER YOU PLEASE
(inspecting a sandwich) WHERE'S THE CHEESE!?!?
DREAMS, THEY'RE GREAT, BUT TELL YA DREAMS WON'T BUY
    YA SOMETHIN' TO EAT
(holding up another sandwich) THAT'S ALL MEAT!!
AS A BOY I DREAMED THAT I WOULD BE THE GREATEST
    BOWLER
OR A DEEP SEA DIVER OR AN AIR TRAFFIC CONTROLLER

(Everything stops for a moment as **CRABBLE** *escapes into his happy memory place. He talks to the audience.)*

And I was! I used to stand in the middle of the planes shouting:

STOP! GO! YIELD! TURN!

And I coulda done it forever.

(A loud crash brings **CRABBLE** *back to reality. He looks behind him and sees* **HAROLD** *picking up a large metal tray he dropped.)*

HAROLD. Sorry…

CRABBLE.
> BUT INSTEAD I WORK A JOB THAT MAKES ME WISH I WERE
>> WHAT WAS DEAD
> BETWEEN BREAD.
> THIS IS MY LIFE NOW
> THIS IS IT

HAROLD.
> AND IT'S HOW IT'S GONNA BE

CRABBLE.
> THIS IS MY LIFE NOW

BOTH.
> YA CAN'T QUIT
> THIS ETERNITY

CRABBLE & HAROLD.
> CAN'T REVERSE IT
> BUT WE CAN CURSE IT

HAROLD.
> SCREW THIS!

CRABBLE.
> LET IT BURN!!!!!!!!

(A surprised look from **HAROLD.** *)*

HAROLD.
> WE COULD PICKET!

CRABBLE.
> GET A ONE-WAY TICKET

CRABBLE & HAROLD.
> AND NEVER
> RETURN!

HAROLD.
> WHO WE KIDDING

CRABBLE.

    THERE AIN'T NO RIDDING

BOTH.

    OF THIS LIVING HELL

CRABBLE. *(gesturing to* **HAROLD***)*

    STUCK WITH THIS PISSER

HAROLD.

    OH GOD, I MISS HER

CRABBLE & HAROLD.

    WHAT'S THAT
    STINK I SMELL?

    THAT STINK'S MY LIFE NOW
    THS IS IT
    THIS IS HOW IT'S GONNA BE
    THIS IS MY LIFE NOW
    YA CAN'T QUIT
    THIS ETERNITY

    WHAT DOES THIS GET US?
    THIS WHOLE LIFE
    THERE'S NO HOPE OF BREAKIN' FREE
    OF MEAT CHEESE AND LETTUCE
    AND REPEAT
    TILL ETERNITY...

    MAYONNAISE MEAT CHEESE 'N LETTUCE
    MAYONNAISE MEAT CHEESE 'N LETTUCE
    MAYONNAISE MEAT CHEESE 'N LETTUCE

    *(***CRABBLE*** grumbles as he exits.)*

NARRATOR. Every evening, after work, Harold comes home just in time to catch:

    *(***DAPHNE*** breezes through.)*

DAPHNE. Rehearsal. Bye!
    (turning back) Oh and your father called again. Call him back, will ya? He's lonely.

HAROLD. OK, I'll call him.

    *(***HAROLD*** moves towards the phone but stops himself.)*

NARRATOR. But Harold doesn't call his father.

Why?

There's no reason and there are a million reasons.

(MR. MCCLAM *enters.*)

[MUSIC #16A: "IN THE OUTER REACHES OF BROOKLYN PART ONE"]

As spring turns to summer, Mr. McClam can be found at home.

Where he sits by the window.

With his record player.

Scene 2.
Mr. McClam and His Record Player (Part 2)

NARRATOR. On the 4th of July, Mr. McClam calls Harold and Daphne to invite them to:

MR. MCCLAM. *(into phone)* Brooklyn for the fireworks.

NARRATOR. But even on a holiday Daphne has:

DAPHNE. Rehearsal. Sorry.

MR. MCCLAM. And Harold?

DAPHNE. Goes to sleep early.

MR. MCCLAM. Oh. Right.

NARRATOR. And so, Mr. McClam heads out to watch the fireworks with his usual boxy companion.

(**MR. MCCLAM** *walks down the street holding his record player.*)

MR. MCCLAM. *(singing)*
LIBIAMO, LIBIAMO, LIBIAMO, LIBIAMO

NARRATOR. When suddenly:

(sound of a car horn)

As he jumps out of the way he loses his balance and sends his record player flying up:

(**MR. MCCLAM** *follows it up with his eyes.*)

It hangs in the air for a glorious instant and then.

(**MR. MCCLAM** *follows it down with his eyes.*)

It falls to the ground and shatters to pieces.
And all Mr. McClam can do is watch.
And then go home.
Where he sits by the window.
Alone.
Staring. And waiting.

(**MR. MCCLAM** *picks up a phone.*)

NARRATOR. And calling.

DAPHNE. Harold, your father called again.

NARRATOR. As summer turns to fall.

DAPHNE. Harold, your father called.

NARRATOR. At first once a day.

DAPHNE. Harold, your father.

NARRATOR. Then once a week.

DAPHNE. Harold, your.

NARRATOR. Then once in a while.

DAPHNE. Harold.

NARRATOR. Then, not at all.

But Harold is too lost in his thoughts of:

HAROLD. Miriam...

(**MIRIAM** *floats through.*)

MIRIAM. You're my soulmate... I think...

NARRATOR. To notice the notable absence of:

DAPHNE. Harold, your father called again.

NARRATOR. Until…

Scene 3.
The Rut

(DAPHNE brings HAROLD coffee and a spoon. She holds up her cup and taps it with her spoon.)

DAPHNE. I'd like to propose a toast! In honor of today being the day before opening night! Or as we show biz folks call it: *Opening Eve.*

(HAROLD half-heartedly toasts with DAPHNE.)

Gosh. Time really flies, huh? November 9th has seemed so far away for so long and now it's / tomorrow.

HAROLD. November 9th?

DAPHNE. Yes.

HAROLD. Tomorrow is –

DAPHNE. November 9th, yes.

HAROLD. Has my father called?

DAPHNE. Not in a few weeks. Harold, what's wrong?
    Is it the coffee? I know it's bad.
    You know who makes the best coffee?
    Miriam.
    Oh Miriam, Miiiriam, Miiiiiiriam...
    I'll never understand why she left New York.
    What could of happened?
    She's so strange!
    I wish she'd just find a nice guy and settle / down –
    (HAROLD throws a spoon hard against the wall.)

HAROLD. *STOP talking about her!*

(A beat. They're both taken aback by this outburst.)

DAPHNE. Harold?

HAROLD. Sorry... I've gotta go to work.

[MUSIC #16B: "ETERNITY (VAMPS)"]

NARRATOR. And so Harold begins his daily march to Sandwiches Sandwiches, a deli outside of which hangs a *sign* that is spelled *correctly.*

(**CRABBLE** *appears, overjoyed.*)

NARRATOR. Yes, after a long and winding tour of the country, I'm happy to report that Crabble's sign finally found its way to New York.

CRABBLE. *(reading the sign)* Sandwiches! *SANDWICHES!!!!* At last!

NARRATOR. At last, Crabble admires the sign over his deli. And for a moment, he feels extremely happy.

But a minute later he's back inside:

CRABBLE.
MAYONNAISE, MEAT, CHEESE 'N LETTUCE
MAYONNAISE, MEAT, CHEESE –

NARRATOR. And then it dawns on him:

CRABBLE. Lightbulbs!

NARRATOR. Yes, for his sign to be truly great it needs:

CRABBLE. Lightbulbs on all four sides!
Ones that blink!

NARRATOR. Needless to say, this involves months of phone calls, miscommunications, and countless anguished cries of:

CRABBLE. *HAROLD!*

NARRATOR. Until, finally, on the same morning that:

DAPHNE. *(tapping her cup)* I'd like to propose a toast!

NARRATOR. Crabble finally flips a switch. And as several dozen bulbs hum to life in the early morning darkness, tears spring to his eyes:

CRABBLE. Oh!

NARRATOR. But just as:

(**HAROLD** *throws his spoon.*)

HAROLD. *(desperate) STOP!* talking about her…

(*We hear the sound of a bulb burning out.*)

NARRATOR. One bulb burns out.

CRABBLE. *Oh for the love of Pete!*

HAROLD. *(to* **DAPHNE***)*

Sorry. I've gotta go to work.

(**DAPHNE** *exits while* **HAROLD** *walks into Sandwiches Sandwiches.*)

CRABBLE.

MAYONNAISE, MEAT, CHEESE 'N LETTUCE.

HAROLD. Hey.

CRABBLE.

MAYONNAISE, MEAT, CHEESE 'N LETTUCE.

HAROLD. Y'know, there's a bulb out on your sign….

CRABBLE. *(beat)* I hate you.

Make a sandwich.

NARRATOR. Harold tries to concentrate on:

HAROLD.

MAYONNAISE MEAT CHEESE…?

CRABBLE. *(annoyed AND shocked)*

'N LETTUCE!

NARRATOR. But he is overcome with a feeling so sad he can hardly stand it. And so he bites the inside of his face, waiting for the feeling to subside. Until…

(**HAROLD** *puts his hand to his mouth.*)

HAROLD. Ow!

CRABBLE. Harold! You're bleeding!

HAROLD. Huh?

CRABBLE. Your face is bleeding all over the provolone! Just STOP.

(**HAROLD** *stops.*)

GO.

(**HAROLD** *turns to leave.*)

I'll clean up after your mess as usual. Oh and pick up a lightbulb on your way into work tomorrow, will ya?

(HAROLD gives a weak thumbs up as he exits.)

CRABBLE. *(to himself)* Yeah he's gonna forget...

(CRABBLE exits.)

NARRATOR. And so Harold leaves work early and heads back to his apartment where an unexpected scene has just begun to unfold...

Scene 4.
A New Ending

*(A manic **JOEY** stands in **DAPHNE**'s living room, dumping out the contents of his bag.)*

DAPHNE. A new ending?

JOEY. Yes!

[MUSIC #17: "I NEED MORE"]

It took eleven months of rehearsal but I think I finally got it right!

(handing her the pages) Now. Full disclosure. You may recognize a few personal details in this song. They say write what you know, so I –

DAPHNE. Do you want to hear it or not?

JOEY. Yes, yes! Sorry.

Please, go on.

DAPHNE.

THERE USED TO BE
A GIRL LIKE ME
WHO LIVED SOME TIME AGO
LIFE WAS MUNDANE
BUT WHY COMPLAIN?
IF THINGS FELT SORT OF SLOW
SHE HAD DAYS OF SUN
STARRED IN PLAYS FOR FUN
AND SHE ALWAYS FELT CARED FOR
AND YET, ONE DAY
I HEARD HER SAY
I NEED MORE

JOEY. So imagine that you're singing this song to a pony.

DAPHNE. A pony?

JOEY. It'll make sense in context, I promise.

So. Singing to a pony. Go.

DAPHNE.

THERE USED TO BE
A GIRL LIKE ME

WHO DARED TO CHASE HER DREAMS
EACH DAY AT NINE
SHE'D STAND IN LINE
HOPE BURSTING AT HER SEAMS
SHE'D SING OUT HER SONG
THEY WOULD SHOUT: "YOU'RE WRONG!"
AND THEN SHOW HER TO THE DOOR.
BUT WITH EACH DEFEAT
SHE'D STILL REPEAT:
I NEED MORE

AND THEN SHE MET A GUY SHE LIKED
A MAN WHO PLAYED GUITAR
HE MADE HER FEEL A LITTLE LESS ALONE
AND THEN SHE GOT A PART IN WHAT WILL HOPEFULLY BE
    A HIT PLAY
IT SEEMED THAT EVERYTHING HAD GONE HER WAY

DAPHNE. Sooo I recognize a *lot* of personal details.

JOEY. I'm sorry. We'll stop.

DAPHNE. No, I want to finish!

JOEY. *(beat)* OK. This last verse is quiet. Your pony's falling asleep.

DAPHNE.

OF COURSE YOU SEE
THAT GIRL IS ME
WHAT LUCK – I SHOULD BE GLAD.
MY JOB'S A JOY
I'VE GOT THE BOY
SO WHY AM I SO SAD?

AND SO WHAT IF HE
BARELY TALKS TO ME
AND EACH KISS FEELS LIKE A CHORE
WHAT DO YOU DO
WHEN DREAMS COME TRUE
BUT YOU NEED MORE.?

I NEED MORE
I NEED MORE

*(**DAPHNE** stares at **JOEY** for a long beat.)*

JOEY. So…the song goes into a scene. She leaves the barn to find a deep-thinking and attractive man observing her from afar. I'll play him.

DAPHNE. Oh, ok…*(reading)* I didn't realize anyone was listening to me.

JOEY. *(off book)* I always listen to you. Your voice is the most beautiful sound in the world.

DAPHNE. I'm engaged.

JOEY. He doesn't know you.

DAPHNE. And you do?

JOEY. Yes.

DAPHNE. *(She looks up nervously.)* Oh. It says that we – did you want to try the –

JOEY. Kiss?

Yes…

If that's ok with you.

DAPHNE. Yes, it seems necessary. To understand the scene.

JOEY. I agree. So. *(clearing his throat)* Good!

    *(Beat. **JOEY** kisses **DAPHNE**.)*

NARRATOR. And it's at *precisely* this point that:

    *(**HAROLD** enters.)*

Harold's instinct is to leave the room immediately – And so he does.

    *(**HAROLD** leaves as **JOEY** and **DAPHNE** break apart.)*

JOEY. And then we hold each other, aand. Lights. Great.

DAPHNE. Was…was that what you wanted me to do? With the kiss? Because I could –

JOEY. No. Yes. That was good. That was perfect.

DAPHNE. This is the final thing you're adding to the show, okay? It's really long as it is –

JOEY. I know, I'm sorry, it's just that – Daphne, I'm going to level with you.

DAPHNE. Don't.

JOEY. *I'm a real mess.* And so is *The Human Condition.* Especially the fourth act. But you – you're not a mess. You're incredible. At everything. And I know I shouldn't be saying this but I can't hold it in anymore, Daphne, I'm in –

(HAROLD opens the door.)

DAPHNE. Harold!

JOEY. Hey, Harbold!

HAROLD. It's Harold.

Harbold isn't even a name.

JOEY. Okay. Well, I'll just be going…

(DAPHNE and HAROLD watch in awkward silence as JOEY spends an unbearably long time gathering up his scattered papers and placing them in his bag. Once JOEY has everything organized, he closes the bag and carefully fastens all of the buckles. Finally, he picks up his fur coat and puts it around his shoulders with dignity. Satisfied, he exits.)

(HAROLD and DAPHNE, finally alone, don't know what to say to each other. HAROLD heads for the bedroom.)

HAROLD. My face is bleeding…

DAPHNE. What happened?

(HAROLD goes into the bedroom. DAPHNE follows him.)

We were just rehearsing.

How was your day?

HAROLD. Fine.

DAPHNE. Good. Hey, after dinner maybe you could play your guitar and I could sing?

HAROLD. I don't think so.

DAPHNE. You never play your guitar anymore.

HAROLD. Mmhm..

DAPHNE. What happened to that song you were writing? About the seahorse?

HAROLD. Sea turtle.

Goodnight.

DAPHNE. Goodnight?

It's only four o'clock.

HAROLD. I'm tired.

DAPHNE. You're going to sleep for fifteen hours?

HAROLD. Guess so.

(After a beat, **DAPHNE** *exits the bedroom.)*

[MUSIC #18: "THE NIGHTMARE"]

NARRATOR. Harold gets in bed while the sun is still out. Hoping to connect with –

HAROLD. Miriam…

NARRATOR. And hours after the sun has set, Daphne makes a bed on the couch. She tries to sleep, but her thoughts keep her awake:

DAPHNE.

I COULD TRY TO FEEL COMPLETE
I COULD JUST WALK OUT THE DOOR
HERE I'LL NEVER FEEL COMPLETE
ALWAYS KNOWING
I NEED MORE

NARRATOR. And Harold closes his eyes only to find that for the first time he is unable to see –

*(***HAROLD*** sits up, distressed.)*

HAROLD. Miriam?

Where'd she go?

NARRATOR. He realizes that Miriam has disappeared from his dreams. He panics.

(music)

He tosses.

(music)

He turns.

(music)

Until…

(**HAROLD**'s *arm shoots out and hits his alarm clock which crashes to the ground.*)

Scene 5.
The Break

NARRATOR. As day breaks, we find ourselves firmly planted in November 9th, 1965. Exactly one year after the sudden death of:

[MUSIC #19: "INTO THE OUTER REACHES OF BROOKLYN PART 2"]

MR. MCCLAM. *(hand on his heart)* Cecily.

NARRATOR. And deep in the outer reaches of Brooklyn, Mr. McClam begins the day by making coffee.

And reading the morning paper.

Which is where he sees:

*(**MR. MCCLAM**'s face lights up.)*

MR. MCCLAM. *(reading) La Traviata!* Playing one night only! Tonight!

NARRATOR. And for the first time in a year he can feel the undeniable presence of:

MR. MCCLAM. *(looking up)* Cecily.

NARRATOR. And so he starts to tell an invisible audience a story:

MR. MCCLAM. *(to **THE NARRATOR**)* You see, the war was over and I was living with my folks. I yelled upstairs –

NARRATOR. Which we don't really have time for right now. Sorry.

MR. MCCLAM. That's ok. Looks like I've got a full day ahead. I need to go change!

NARRATOR. Meanwhile, across the river, instead of waking up at 7:30 a.m. to the sound of his alarm clock.

Harold wakes up at 10 a.m. to –

*(**HAROLD**'s phone rings. He awakes with a start and picks up his phone.)*

HAROLD. Hello?

CRABBLE. Harold, it's 10 a.m!

HAROLD. I must have overslept.

(**HAROLD** *bends down and picks up his clock.*)

My clock broke.

(**HAROLD** *stares at his clock.*)

NARRATOR. And he can't help but take the path and make the connection:

HAROLD. *This is what it looks like when time stops...*

CRABBLE. What? You've got exactly ten minutes to get down here, Harold! Ten minutes and then –

NARRATOR. And then –

CRABBLE. And *then* –

HAROLD. I quit!

CRABBLE. Excuse me?!

HAROLD. I quit!

CRABBLE. Very funny. Now you need to get out of bed and get on the train, Harold.
GET ON THE TRAIN!

HAROLD. The train!

CRABBLE. Get on it!

(**HAROLD** *hangs up the phone, exhilarated.*)

HAROLD. I need to get on the train!

[MUSIC #20: "AT LEAST I'LL KNOW I TRIED"]

(**HAROLD** *gets up, resolved.*)

OK.

(**HAROLD** *gets his guitar, looks around.*)

OK!

(**HAROLD** *grabs the broken alarm clock and heads out the bedroom. In the living room he sees* **DAPHNE** *on the couch, awake.*)

DAPHNE. Hey.

HAROLD. Hey.

So, I'm going.

DAPHNE. I see that.

Well, have a good day.

HAROLD. You too.

(The stage shifts and becomes a big open space. The characters cross the stage, each beginning his/her day.)

NARRATOR.

INSTANTS, MOMENTS
ONE FLICKERING FLAME OF LIGHT

(spoken) There are rhythms in our bodies.
Some of them we invent slowly for ourselves, over time.

*(**CRABBLE** heads to the deli.)*

CRABBLE.

MAYONNAISE, MEAT, CHEESE 'N LETTUCE.
MAYONNAISE, MEAT, CHEESE 'N LETTUCE.

NARRATOR. Some we adopt to distract ourselves.

*(**DAPHNE** paces in her apartment.)*

DAPHNE. Unique New York. Unique New York. Unique New York. Unique New York.

NARRATOR. Some we use to remember.

*(**MR. MCCLAM** walks down his stoop. He wears an overcoat and a tuxedo.)*

MR. MCCLAM.

LIBIAMO, LIBIAMO NE'LIETI CALICI

NARRATOR. And some we use to move ourselves forward.

*(**HAROLD** strums his guitar as he walks with purpose.)*

HAROLD.

I FINALLY KNOW WHERE I AM GOING
THERE ISN'T A SHADOW OF DOUBT
THERE'S NO TIME TO PACK, AND THERE'S NO LOOKING
    BACK
WHAT ADDRESS? WELL I GUESS I'LL FIND OUT

MR. MCCLAM.

FINDING I'M TIRED OF WISHING
FROM UNDER A LAYER OF FROST
MY LIFE ISN'T DONE, IT COULD JUST USE SOME SUN
WHAT'S TO LOSE?

HAROLD.

I REFUSE TO GET LOST

HAROLD & MR. MCCLAM.

THERE IS LIFE
SO MUCH LIFE

HAROLD.

AND MY LIFE'S NOT A WASTE
IT'S JUST BEEN MISPLACED
NOW IT'S ALMOST AS IF
I'M ON TOP OF A CLIFF
WHERE THE VIEW STRETCHES OUT FAR AND WIDE
MY HEART MIGHT BREAK
THAT'S A CHANCE I GOTTA TAKE
AND AT LEAST I'LL KNOW I TRIED

MR. MCCLAM.

MY FOOT IS INFLAMED WITH ARTHRITIS
FROM THE HEEL TO THE TIP OF THE TOE
SO WHAT IF IT LIMPS, I'LL AT LEAST GET A GLIMPSE
OF A MEM'RY FROM LONG, LONG AGO

WHEN THE ORCHESTRA THUNDERED WITH MUSIC
AND A GIRL WHO'S TOO GOOD TO BE TRUE
BUT I HAVE TO WAIT FOR THE DISCOUNTED RATE
BECAUSE SEATS ARE EXPENSIVE –

(The **CUSTOMER** *ahead of* **MR. MCCLAM** *approaches the box office.)*

NARRATOR/CUSTOMER. I'll take two.

NARRATOR/TICKET SELLER. Last two. We're all sold out, folks!

MR. MCCLAM.

YOU'VE GOT NERVE
DON'T I DESERVE TO HEAR…

*(***MCCLAM** *closes his eyes and hears* La Traviata.*)*

NARRATOR/TICKET SELLER. I'm sorry, sir.

MR. MCCLAM.

I ASSUME

THERE'S STANDING ROOM OR...

NARRATOR/TICKET SELLER. If there was a ticket, I'd sell it to you.

MR. MCCLAM.

I'M AN OLD MAN

NOT SOME SNOBBY –

LET ME LISTEN

FROM THE LOBBY

NARRATOR/TICKET SELLER.

CAN'T BLOCK THE EXITS

I'M SORRY, GOOD DAY TO YOU

SORRY I WISH I COULD HELP

MMMMM...

NARRATOR. And as Mr. McClam tells a ticket seller:

MR. MCCLAM. Goodbye.

NARRATOR. Harold tells a ticket seller:

HAROLD. Hello!

ONE-WAY PLEASE TO SOUTH DAKOTA

SO I CAN KNOW I'M ALIVE

SO I CAN FEEL, SOMETHING TRUE, SOMETHING REAL

NARRATOR/TICKET SELLER.

HERE YOU GO; IT COSTS TEN TWENTY-FIVE...

NARRATOR. As Harold waits for the train, Mr. McClam retreats back home.

MR. MCCLAM. Cecily...

NARRATOR. And as Mr. McClam retreats, Joey Storms sits in his office trying to type:

JOEY. One more scene!

NARRATOR. And as Joey types, Daphne prepares to head to the theater. But when she picks up her purse, she realizes:

DAPHNE. *(looking at the bag)* I need more.

NARRATOR. And as Daphne packs a bigger bag, Crabble gets ready to face the lunch rush alone:

CRABBLE. Here we go...
MAYONNAISE, MEAT CHEESE 'N LETTUCE
MAYONNAISE, MEAT CHEESE 'N LETTUCE

CRABBLE.	MR. MCCLAM.
MAYONNAISE, MEAT CHEESE 'N LETTUCE MAYONNAISE, MEAT CHEESE 'N LETTUCE	CECILY....

CRABBLE.	MR. MCCLAM.	DAPHNE.
MAYONNAISE, MEAT CHEESE 'N LETTUCE	CECILY...	I NEED MORE

CRABBLE.	MR. MCCLAM.	DAPHNE.	HAROLD.
MAYONNAISE, MEAT CHEESE 'N LETTUCE	CECILY...	I NEED MORE	AND AT LEAST I'LL KNOW I TRIED

CRABBLE.	MR. MCCLAM.	DAPHNE.	HAROLD.
(repeating)	*(repeating)*	*(repeating)*	*(repeating)*
MAYONNAISE, MEAT CHEESE 'N LETTUCE...	CECILY....	I NEED MORE...	AND AT LEAST I'LL KNOW I TRIED...

JOEY. *(overlapping with above)*
THIS ISN'T RIGHT EVERYTHING'S WRONG
I NEED MORE TIME ANOTHER SONG
ONE FINAL TRY

NARRATOR. Harold's train finally arrives and he races to the platform:

HAROLD.
GOODBYE NEW YORK, SEE YOU LATER
THE COUNTRY IS WHERE I BELONG
NO HONKING CARS, ONLY QUIET AND STARS
AND THE GIRL WHO FIRST SANG ME THIS SONG

EVERYONE.
> LA DA DA DA DA DA DA DA DA
> LA DA DA DA DA DA DA DA DA

HAROLD.
> TRAIN, DON'T DELAY
> TAKE ME AWAY
> I'M A MAN ON A QUEST
> ALL THE SIGNS POINT TO WEST
> BECAUSE DESTINY CAN'T BE DENIED
> IT MIGHT BE ROUGH
> BUT ENOUGH IS ENOUGH
> AND AT LEAST I'LL KNOW I TRIED
> YEAH AT LEAST I'LL KNOW I TRIED

Scene 6.
The Train Station

NARRATOR. Harold is about to get on the train, when he can sense that he is being watched.

And so he turns around, and there, on the opposite track, he sees:

(**MIRIAM** *enters.*)

HAROLD. Miriam?!

(**MIRIAM** *and* **HAROLD** *lock eyes.*)

Wait right there! Don't move!
Seriously!

(**HAROLD** *runs off to cross platforms.*)

NARRATOR. Why is Miriam back in New York?

To find out we must take one brief and final detour back to Hill City. Where two days earlier, out of the blue –

(**MIRIAM** *is nervously knitting when her phone rings. It startles her and she gasps.*)

MIRIAM.*(answering the phone, tentatively)* Hellooo?

DAPHNE. Miriam?

MIRIAM. *(scared whisper)* Who is this?

DAPHNE. It's Daphne. Are you okay? You sound like you're hiding.

MIRIAM. Hiding? Ha! No, I'm feeling great! And so calm! I've been knitting!

(**MIRIAM** *stabs a big knot of yarn with knitting needles.*)

DAPHNE. So, my show is opening in two days. And I really need someone to be there.

MIRIAM. What about Harold?

DAPHNE. I don't know if he'll come.

Things between us aren't…they're bad.

But I can't think about that right now. Will you come to New York?

MIRIAM. I can't. I can't go back to New York. I'm / sorry.

DAPHNE. Please? The show's a mess. I'm scared.

MIRIAM. Don't be. You're a star.

DAPHNE. I wish I had my lucky ring.

MIRIAM. A-ha! I thought you didn't believe in that kind of thing!

DAPHNE. *(chuckling)* I miss you, Miriam.

MIRIAM. I miss you too.

Break a leg, sis. I love you.

DAPHNE. Love you too.

NARRATOR. Miriam hangs up the phone with Daphne and is torn.

[MUSIC #20A: "STARS, I TRUST (REPRISE)"]

*(**MIRIAM** goes outside and sits on her swing.)*

MIRIAM. *(to herself)* What do I do?

NARRATOR. Ever since she ran away from New York, Miriam's life has been ruled by her fear of:

MIRIAM. Claiming my destiny.

(a la the **GYPSY***) ALL. OF. IT.*

NARRATOR. But as she stares at the shapeless blob she's been knitting for months, she realizes:

MIRIAM. I can't live like this. Afraid all the time.

NARRATOR. And so she does her best to recall:

*(**NARRATOR** hands **MIRIAM** the astronomy book.)*

(as **FATHER***)* I think I've got something that'll protect us both from our fears. Read that.

*(**MIRIAM** reads and looks up at the sky.)*

MIRIAM. *(singing)*
DEAR TINY DOTS OF TWINKLING LIGHT

NARRATOR. And that's when she makes the decision:

MIRIAM. I'll go back to New York and give Daphne her lucky ring. And then I'll immediately turn around and come home. What could be scary about that?

*(**HAROLD** bounds down the platform, giddy.)*

HAROLD. Miriam!

MIRIAM. *(muttering to herself, terrified)* Oh no.

HAROLD. Hi! It's really you! I can't believe it! But also, I can believe it! Because:

*(**HAROLD** waves around the broken clock.)*

This is what it looks like when time stops!

[MUSIC #21: "ME WITH YOU"]

MIRIAM. What?

HAROLD. The signs! They're adding up, all of them!
The question. And the song. And I've got some theories about 5, 2, 7 –

MIRIAM. Harold –

HAROLD. And this! You show up just as I'm getting on a train to go find you! That's gotta be a sign!

MIRIAM. Find me, why?

HAROLD.

I DON'T KNOW IF THERE'S LUCK OR FATE
I MIGHT DEBATE THAT THERE COULD BE
A DESTINY

MIRIAM. I'm just here to bring Daphne her lucky ring.

HAROLD.

WHO KNOWS IF THERE'S A GRAND DESIGN
A COSMIC PLAN OR GOD DIVINE
IN WHAT WE SEE

THERE'S ONLY ONE THING THAT I KNOW IS TRUE
THAT'S ME WITH YOU.
WITH –

MIRIAM. *Daphne.*

HAROLD. Daphne and I are finished! We should've broken up by now but she was always at rehearsal and I could barely get out of bed and I wanted to go find you but –

I WAS AFRAID, I DIDN'T KNOW
I THOUGHT YOU HATED ME
AND SO, I LET IT GO

MIRIAM. I never hated you.

HAROLD. Good! 'Cause –

    I NEVER DREAMED THAT I COULD FEEL
    A GREAT DEAL BETTER THAN JUST FINE.
    YOU WERE THE SIGN
    WHAT WOKE ME UP FROM ALL I EVER KNEW
    WAS ME WITH YOU.
    WITH –

MIRIAM. I can't do this.

    It's not just about Daphne.

    I have a *mountain life,* OK? Do you know what a mountain life is?

HAROLD. Is that like with goats?

MIRIAM. No. It's a life that goes up, up, up…and then DOWN. The psychic saw it! She said I'm fated to have a *great fall!*

HAROLD. What does that mean?

MIRIAM. A sudden death! What else could it mean?

HAROLD. I don't know. Maybe she meant you were going to have a great fall. Like the season. Like, ooh, look at the leaves, what a *great fall!*

MIRIAM. That's *not* what she meant. I checked. She said I'm going to have a love affair with my soulmate *and* I'm going to have a great fall. *AND* there's no way to stop it from happening.

HAROLD. Let me get this straight:

    THERE'S NO WAY TO STOP THE FALL?

MIRIAM.

    SHE SAID NO, THERE'S NONE AT ALL

HAROLD.

    WELL OKAY, THAT MEANS YOU'RE FREE

MIRIAM.

    THAT'S NOT TRUE, HOW CAN THAT BE?

HAROLD.

I MEAN JUST DO WHAT MAKES YOU HAPPY IF YOU CAN'T
   CONTROL YOUR FATE

MIRIAM.

NO YOU DON'T GET IT, SHE SAID IT –

HAROLD.

I GET IT, I DO –

MIRIAM.

NO YOU –

HAROLD.

NO YOU SHOULD JUST DO WHAT YOU WANNA DO
HEY, YOU WANNA GRAB A BITE?

MIRIAM.

I HAVE DAPHNE'S SHOW TONIGHT

HAROLD.

THAT'S TONIGHT BUT THAT'S NOT NOW

MIRIAM.

THIS IS CRAZY ANYHOW

HAROLD.

WE WON'T KNOW UNTIL WE'VE / TRIED

MIRIAM.

SO WE SHOULD DECIDE TO RIDE OFF INTO THE SUNSET? /
   HOW COULD I – ?

HAROLD.

IF I WERE YOU I THINK I'D
FORGET ALL FEAR – JUST LET YOURSELF AGREE
TO BE WITH ME

Have lunch with me.

There's a great Chinese food place around the corner.

MIRIAM. *(holding up the clock)* I can't. The signs are adding
   up! Your clock broke! You said it!

HAROLD. Forget what I said!

SOMETIMES A BUSTED, BROKEN CLOCK
IS JUST A BUSTED, BROKEN CLOCK
COME TAKE A WALK

MIRIAM. I'd love to but –

HAROLD.

IF FATE'S NOT WRITTEN IN THE STARS
THAT MEANS IT'S OURS TO MAKE – LET'S WALK
JUST DOWN THE BLOCK
'CAUSE THERE ARE OTHER DAYS FOR DYIN'

MIRIAM.

HOW COULD WE GO?

HAROLD.

AND SO WHAT IF AT LOVE WE'RE ROOKIES
IT'S LUNCHTIME AND I'M BUYIN'

MIRIAM.

OH, HAROLD

HAROLD.

LET'S LEAVE THE FORTUNES TO THE COOKIES
(spoken) Just one lunch. And then we can part ways
forever.

That's hardly a love affair.

Whattaya say?

MIRIAM. Well, I *am* hungry.

HAROLD. Is that a yes?

MIRIAM. And you can't get good lo mein in South Dakota.

And I suppose I have time to…

FIND SOMEWHERE WARM, AND FOR AN HOUR OR TWO

MIRIAM & HAROLD.

JUST BE
WITH YOU

*(**HAROLD** offers **MIRIAM** his hand and she takes it.
They exit together.)*

Scene 7.
Time Stops

[MUSIC #21A: "WHAT COMES NEXT"]

NARRATOR. As evening sets in Daphne stands onstage in an empty theater.

DAPHNE. *(looking out, excited)* Soon all of those seats are going to have people in them!

(She notices JOEY off to the side, typing furiously.)

What are you doing?

JOEY. Writing one more scene!

DAPHNE. You have to stop!

NARRATOR. And deep in the outer reaches of Brooklyn, Mr. McClam finds himself in a pawn shop:

MR. MCCLAM. Yes, I'd like to trade this wedding band for a record player?

NARRATOR/PAWN SHOP OWNER. This is a solid gold ring. You could get a lot more for it. You want a washer dryer? Mahogany dining room set?

MR. MCCLAM. Just a record player, please.

(NARRATOR hands over a record player to MR. MCCLAM. He exits as CRABBLE appears in the deli.)

NARRATOR. And the sun is just beginning to set when:

CRABBLE.
MAYONNAISE MEAT –
(looking up at a clock) 5 p.m.! Quitting time!

NARRATOR. Crabble puts on his coat and heads out the door, above which sits a sign that still contains:

CRABBLE. A dead bulb!

NARRATOR. Which was supposed to be replaced by:

CRABBLE. *Harold!*

NARRATOR. Who, is just finishing up a three-hour lunch with –

HAROLD. Miriam –

(HAROLD and MIRIAM enter.)

MIRIAM. I can't believe it's so late! I need to get Daphne her ring!

(HAROLD stops walking.)

HAROLD. Um…lunch is technically over.

And I'm a man of my word.

So, I guess this is where we part ways forever.

MIRIAM. Oh.

Right.

Well, maybe you could just walk me to the theater first? I tend to get lost.

HAROLD. Happy to help.

(HAROLD and MIRIAM exit.)

NARRATOR. And as Harold and Miriam walk to the theater, across the river Mr. McClam sits inside his apartment. He watches through the window as the sun sinks below the horizon. And as the last bit of light slips away:

(MR. MCCLAM stares at the record player.)

MR. MCCLAM. Cecily…

NARRATOR. And as Crabble walks into a hardware store:

CRABBLE. One lightbulb, please!

NARRATOR. And as Joey continues to type:

JOEY. One more line!

DAPHNE. We open in less than three hours!

NARRATOR. And as Harold and Miriam approach the theater:

HAROLD. OK. This is it.

MIRIAM. Yes.

Well, thank you.

NARRATOR. Mr. McClam begins to draw a bath.

(A tub appears.)

HAROLD. I had a great time.

MIRIAM. Me too.

NARRATOR. He waits for the water to rise.

(MR. MCCLAM *runs the water.*)

HAROLD. Goodbye forever.

MIRIAM. Goodbye forever.

NARRATOR. He steps into the tub.

(MR. MCCLAM *steps into the tub, fully clothed.*)

HAROLD. I'm going now.

MIRIAM. OK.

(HAROLD *turns around and walks away.*)

NARRATOR. He plugs in his record player.

(MR. MCCLAM *plugs in the record player.*)

And he gathers the courage to do what comes next while:

(JOEY *types.*)

DAPHNE. Stop writing!

JOEY. One more word!

NARRATOR. And just as:

(CRABBLE *climbs a ladder to his sign, holding a lightbulb.*)

CRABBLE. *(screwing in the bulb)* A-ha!

(HAROLD *is almost gone when* MIRIAM *shouts to him…*)

MIRIAM. Wait!

(HAROLD *turns around.*)

NARRATOR. And only a moment after:

(MR. MCCLAM *takes a deep breath.*)

MR. MCCLAM. Forgive me, Harold.

NARRATOR. And at the exact instant that:

MIRIAM. *(running to* HAROLD*)* Don't go!

(MR. MCCLAM *drops the record player in the tub.*)

(HAROLD *and* MIRIAM *kiss.*)

(*Blackout.*)

NARRATOR. Time stops.

Scene 8.
The Blackout

(**NARRATOR** *illuminates his face with a lighter.*)

NARRATOR. On the evening of November 9th, 1965 at approximately half past five.

Time stops.

And for many years after many smart people will look back and try to figure out what went wrong. And there will be theories. But no one will know exactly where it began. In the end they'll have to settle for the plain but indisputable fact that you can't have the lights without also having:

MIRIAM. A blackout!

HAROLD. OK, so this *definitely* could be what it looks like when:

HAROLD, MIRIAM, NARRATOR. Time stops.

NARRATOR. And throughout the Northeast.

Theaters go dark.

JOEY. Are you *flipping* kidding me?! *(to* **DAPHNE***)* Stay here – I'll be back!

NARRATOR. And bulbs hum to sleep.

CRABBLE. *(looking at his bulb in disbelief)* No.

Did I break the city?

NARRATOR. And turntables stop turning.

MR. MCCLAM. *(looking up)* Cecily?

[MUSIC #21B "TIME STOPS"]

NARRATOR. But as one system fails.

Another is revealed.

Here in the city, we live under an ever-thickening curtain of man-made light.

What we're used to thinking of as darkness –

Is actually a haze.

But there are moments when the haze lifts.

(Stars begin to emerge. As the **NARRATOR** *continues they expand and grow in number until the space is flooded with points of light. A gesture towards the overwhelming nature of a clear night sky.)*

NARRATOR. And we're reminded that there's an entire galaxy stretching out above us.

That we're surrounded by something that's impossible to comprehend.

Or control.

HAROLD. *(looking up) Whoa...* *(to* **MIRIAM***)* Are you like, totally spooked?

MIRIAM. No.

I'm not scared anymore.

*(***MIRIAM*** takes a book out of her pocket.)*

Read that.

HAROLD. *(reading)* "Nearly all of the elements that make up Earth and its life forms were created inside the heart of a dying star, as it exploded out into the atmosphere."

MIRIAM. It's my father's book. I take it everywhere I go. Is that weird?

*(***HAROLD*** touches his mother's guitar and smiles.)*

HAROLD. No. It's not.

(They kiss.)

NARRATOR. On November 9th 1965.

As theaters go dark.

And bulbs hum to sleep.

And turntables stop turning.

People get up out of their chairs, couches, bathtubs...

*(***MR. MCCLAM*** gets up.)*

And go outside.

And mill about.

And talk to people they haven't talked to in years.

Neighbors who remark:

NARRATOR. *(to* **MR. MCCLAM***)* "Sharp tuxedo."

And, "How's your son?"

And, "Your clothes are all wet. You're gonna catch pneumonia!"

And as a coat is draped over Mr. McClam's shoulders he hears: "I have a record player just like that one."

MR. MCCLAM. Really? Do you happen to have a recording of *La Traviata*?

NARRATOR. As a matter of fact, I do.

MR. MCCLAM. Can I borrow it?

NARRATOR. Sure.

(**MR. MCCLAM** *hugs him.*)

MR. MCCLAM. Thank you!

NARRATOR. You really like *La Traviata*, huh?

MR. MCCLAM. It's my favorite.

NARRATOR. Why?

MR. MCCLAM. You really want to know?

NARRATOR. Yes.

MR. MCCLAM. *Really?*

(**HAROLD** *and* **MIRIAM** *sit down on a bench.*)

MIRIAM. I think this is the happiest day of my life.

HAROLD. Me too. Which is funny because exactly one year ago today was the saddest day of my life because my mom died… Way to ruin the mood, Harold. Sorry, I don't know why I –

MIRIAM. What was she like?

HAROLD. My mom? Well…

(**MR. MCCLAM** *and* **NARRATOR** *sit on the stoop.*)

MR. MCCLAM. OK, then…*(clearing his throat)*…

[MUSIC #22: "CECILY SMITH"]

HAROLD. *(to* **MIRIAM***)* There's this story my dad likes to tell…

MR. MCCLAM. *(to* **NARRATOR***)* It's a good story.

HAROLD. Or my mom liked to hear him tell it…

MR. MCCLAM.

THE WAR WAS OVER
I WAS LIVIN' WITH MY FOLKS
I YELLED UPSTAIRS, "HEY MA,
I'M OFF TO GRAB SOME SMOKES."
AND MY FATHER CALLED, "WHY YOU NEED TO SMOKE SO
    LATE?"
I'D LIED
I HAD A DATE

FREE OF MY FOLKS' ENSLAVEMENT
SKIPPIN' ALONG THE PAVEMENT
TO SEE A BRUNETTE
WHO I NEVER MET
BUT I NEVER WOULD FORGET

HOW SHE LOOKED IN THAT DRESS
HOW SHE STUCK OUT HER HAND AND SAID
"MY NAME IS CECILY SMITH
AND I HOPE YOU LIKE MUSIC

'CAUSE I'VE GOT TWO
TICKETS FOR *LA*
TRAVIATA "
THAT'S WHEN I SAID
"I HATE OPERA"

SHE LAUGHED AND SAID
"WELL LUCKY FOR YOU
THAT YOU'RE WITH CECILY SMITH
WHO CARES WHAT YOU
ARE LISTENING TO
IT'S WHO YOU'RE LISTENING WITH"

WE TAKE OUR SEATS
HER HANDS ARE FOLDED IN HER LAP
IF NOT A KISS, THEN
I AT LEAST WILL GET A NAP
SO I CLOSE MY EYES AS THE ORCHESTRA BEGINS
THEN I
HEAR VIOLINS

AND THE HAIR ON MY NECK WAS RISING
A FEELING NEW AND SURPRISING
BUT IT WASN'T THE SOUND
THAT MADE MY HEART POUND
NO, IT WAS BECAUSE I FOUND

THAT HER HAND IS IN MINE
AND THAT'S WHERE IT WILL STAY
UNTIL THEY PLAY THE FINAL CHORD
SHE SAYS, "WERE YOU BORED?"

AND I SAY,
"I GUESS IT WASN'T
QUITE SO BAD."
IT WAS THE BEST TIME
THAT I EVER HAD.

SHE LAUGHED AND SAID
"WELL LUCKY FOR YOU
I GOT SEATS TO BEETHOVEN'S FIFTH."
WHO CARES WHAT YOU
ARE LISTENING TO
IT'S WHO YOU'RE LISTENING WITH

A PERFECT WIFE
A PERFECT LIFE

TIME EXPLODED
LIKE A BULLET FROM A GUN
A WEEK, A YEAR
AND THEN A MARRIAGE AND A SON
AND A RENTAL WHERE I STILL CAN HEAR HER LAUGH
WHEN I PLAY
THE PHONOGRAPH

AND I LET THE MUSIC GUIDE ME
AND CECILY SITS BESIDE ME
A GIRL OF NINETEEN
WITH A NERVOUS MARINE
FEEL HER HEAD BEGIN TO LEAN

AS THE MELODY SOARS
AND THOUGH IT WAS REAL

IT DOESN'T FEEL LIKE IT COULD BE
THAT NIGHT WHEN YOU SAID TO ME

"I'VE GOT TWO
TICKETS FOR *LA
TRAVIATA*"…
IT'S SAD BUT TRUE
HOW MUCH I MISS YOU
I MISS YOU, CECILY SMITH
LIFE IS NOT THE THINGS THAT WE DO
IT'S WHO WE'RE DOING THEM WITH

NARRATOR. As Mr. McClam sits on his stoop, telling his story, he sees a raised hand in the audience:

MR. MCCLAM. Question?

NARRATOR. What's *La Traviata?*

MR. MCCLAM. It's a three act opera by Giuseppe Verdi. A tragedy that centers around a love triangle between –

NARRATOR. No, I mean, like how does it go?

MR. MCCLAM. Oh. Well… It goes like this:

[MUSIC #22A: "LIBIAMO"]

LIBIAMO, LIBIAMO NE'LIETE CALICI
CHE LA BELLEZA INFIORA
E LA FUGEVOL, FUGGOVOL ORA S'INNEBRIIA VOLUTA

NARRATOR.

As Mr. McClam sings, a crowd of people will gather to watch and listen.
And they will tell their children who will tell their children about the night they watched a man sing an entire opera by himself.

MR. MCCLAM.
(underneath)
LIBIAMO NE'DOLCI FREMITI
CHE SUCITA L'AMORE,
POICHE QUELL'OCHIO AL CORE OMNIPOTENTE VA
LIBIAMO, AMORE
AMOR FRAI CALICI PIU CALDIBACI A VRA.

*(**MR. MCCLAM** crosses off singing as **CRABBLE** appears on top of a ladder with a flashlight.)*

NARRATOR. Meanwhile, across the river, Crabble looks down at the traffic jam on the streets below.

(horns honking)

CRABBLE. Idiots! Shut up already! You've never been in a power failure before? Geez! Just take turns at the intersection and –
(realizing) Oh my god. Wait a minute!

(CRABBLE *excitedly descends the ladder and runs into the street. He waves his arms, yelling at the cars.)*

CRABBLE. *(cont.)* Stop! Go! Yield! Turn!
Stop! Go! Yield! Turn!
Stop! Go! Yield! Turn!

NARRATOR. And as the cars begin to flow into an organized stream, Crabble stops an old brown station wagon with busted headlights:

CRABBLE. Hey Buddy! Your lights are out!

NARRATOR/DRIVER. I know, I wasn't gonna drive this car! But the trains are down! And my old lady's stuck in the basement at Macy's!

CRABBLE. Alright, just be careful!

(NARRATOR/DRIVER *sticks his head out of the window.)*

NARRATOR/DRIVER. Anthony?? Anthony Marshall? Is that you?!

(CRABBLE *shines a flashlight at the car.)*

CRABBLE. Frankie Correnti?
I haven't seen you in ages!

NARRATOR/DRIVER. Crazy night, huh!?

(car honking)

NARRATOR & CRABBLE. *(shout back at the cars)* Alright!

CRABBLE. Good to see ya.

NARRATOR/DRIVER. You keep up the good work!

CRABBLE. *(beaming with pride)* Thanks, Frankie.

NARRATOR. And while improvised performances begin…

(**CRABBLE** *walks off conducting the traffic.*)

NARRATOR. ...Scheduled performances are cancelled.

And as eight o'clock rolls around, theaters are dark and empty.

Except one...

(**DAPHNE** *enters and sits.*)

Where Daphne sits.

On the edge of the stage.

In the same place she's been sitting since the lights went out.

(**JOEY** *enters, shining a flashlight around.*)

JOEY. *Daphne!*

DAPHNE. *(jumping up)* Joey! Where have you been? Look, don't panic. We'll just open the show tomorrow night. And we can use the extra time to polish the sections that need work. *(starting to warm up)* I'll start warming up and we'll get to work / on the –

JOEY. I'm cancelling the show.

DAPHNE. No you're not. Unique / New York.

JOEY. Yes, I am. I should've done this months ago. But I didn't have the courage. I –

DAPHNE. We should rehearse the new song. What's my first note?

JOEY. Daphne. The New York City sky is filled with stars for the first time.

And you're trapping yourself in here in the dark.

And it's my fault.

DAPHNE. Big deal. I've seen stars before. I'm from a small town with no pollution.

JOEY. But you haven't seen anything like this. Come outside.

DAPHNE. I don't want to go outside, okay? I want to work.

(She begins to warm up her voice.)

JOEY. Listen to me, the show / is over!

DAPHNE. No! You're not pulling the plug because of a little technical problem!

JOEY. A little technical problem? They're saying on the radio that a giant power outage hit all of the states in the Northeast. A grid overloaded up north. Near Lake Ontario! In Canada! I've never been to Canada!

DAPHNE. Oh god, you're having nervous breakdown.

JOEY. No, I'm finally starting to feel calm. I was standing out there. Looking up at the sky. And I had an epiphany:

There are so many things I've never seen!

I need to leave the city where I was born.

And go out into the *world*.

Climb the mountains of Switzerland.

Trek across the deserts of Africa.

See the Electric Generators of Canada.

Will you come with me?

DAPHNE. Are you serious?

JOEY. Yes!

(After a beat, DAPHNE grabs her suitcase.)

DAPHNE. Okay. Well this is actually perfect because I'm already packed.

I decided this morning. I'm leaving Harold.

So I'm ready to go. With you.

JOEY. Daphne!

(JOEY rushes to DAPHNE and they kiss.)

I feel like spinning you! *(He spins her.)* You're so light! Like a napkin!

(JOEY holds out his hand to DAPHNE.)

Come outside.

[MUSIC #23: "THE GREAT FALL"]

(They walk outside and look up.)

DAPHNE. *(breathless)* Oh...

(They stand there for a moment.)

I can't leave.

JOEY. What? Yes you can, c'mon!

DAPHNE. No. I've dreamed of getting here my whole life.

I can't leave.

JOEY. *(beat)* I understand.

But I need to go now or I'll never do it.

I'll be back.

I don't know when.

But I'll probably have a really big beard.

DAPHNE. *(smiles, a beat)* Goodbye, Joey.

JOEY. Goodbye, Daphne.

(**JOEY** *takes her hand and kisses it.* **JOEY** *fades into the crowd as* **DAPHNE** *takes in the scene around her.*)

Scene 9.
The Great Fall

NARRATOR. On November 9th, 1965, a tear in the fabric of time becomes a window into another way of life. As people step outside they find themselves transformed into guests at an impromptu party to which thirty million people have been invited. It's easy to get lost in the crowd. A comfort, even.

(**DAPHNE** *disappears into the crowd.*)

A giddy sense of freedom hangs over the city like a magic cloak.

It can't last.

Everyone knows that.

And so they make the most of it while they can.

(**HAROLD** *and* **MIRIAM** *appear.* **HAROLD** *plays his guitar.*)

HAROLD.

DOESN'T MATTER WHAT WE DO

MIRIAM.

SEE THOSE STARS

HAROLD.

I JUST NEED TO BE WITH YOU

MIRIAM.

GLOWING

HAROLD & MIRIAM.

LA DA DA DA DA DA DA DA

(*They kiss.*)

MIRIAM. Let's go somewhere. Anywhere.

HAROLD. Like, run away?

MIRIAM. Yeah.

HAROLD. Where do you want to go?

MIRIAM. (*thinks, then…*) The ocean!

HAROLD. You wanna go to the ocean?

Then I'm taking you to the ocean!

NARRATOR. On November 9th, 1965.

> As theaters go dark.
>
> And bulbs hum to sleep.
>
> And turntables stop turning.
>
> And the city becomes a party.
>
> Harold and Miriam run.

*(**HAROLD** and **MIRIAM** start to run away.)*

MIRIAM. Wait! Daphne needs her lucky ring!

*(**MIRIAM** shows **HAROLD** the ring. He takes it.)*

HAROLD. Don't worry! We'll mail it to her!

*(**HAROLD** puts the ring in his pocket.)*

> Now, come on! I'm pretty sure the ocean is this way! Eventually!

NARRATOR. Miriam is about to follow Harold when she looks up and sees a giant clock stuck at:

MIRIAM. *(breathless)* 5:27

NARRATOR. She stops in her tracks and wonders – could it really be?

NARRATOR & MIRIAM. Did time stop at 5, 2, 7?

NARRATOR. And for a split second Harold is too busy running and singing:

HAROLD.

> LA DA DA DA DA DA DA DA

NARRATOR. To notice anything. He doesn't notice –

*(**DAPHNE** appears.)*

DAPHNE. Harold?

NARRATOR. And he doesn't notice that Miriam is standing in the middle of the street, when a car with busted headlights flies around the corner and –

(We hear a car speeding.)

MIRIAM. *(looking at the clock, amazed)* Harold!

DAPHNE. Miriam?

HAROLD. *(turning around)* Daphne?

(We hear the car screech to a halt as **MIRIAM** *gasps.)*

HAROLD & DAPHNE. Miriam!!!

(Everything stops. A long beat.)

[MUSIC #24: "FLY BY NIGHT (REPRISE)"]

NARRATOR. Our story tonight circles around a triangle. Composed of two women.

*(***MIRIAM*** and* **DAPHNE** *step forward.)*

And one man.

*(***HAROLD*** steps forward.)*

That is until it straightens out.

(The **NARRATOR** *puts his hand on* **MIRIAM***'s shoulder. They share a look of understanding. She leaves the stage.)*

And becomes a line.

DA DA DA DA DA DA DA DA DA DA
DA DA DA DA DA DA DA DA DA
DA DA DA DA DA DA DA DA DA DA
DA DA DA DA DA DA DA DA DA

*(***HAROLD*** and* **DAPHNE** *sit down in a hospital waiting room.)*

Harold and Daphne sit in a dark emergency room for what seems like an eternity.

HAROLD. *(noticing)* A suitcase?

DAPHNE. *(looking away)* Oh… Yeah.

HAROLD. *(holding out the ring to* **DAPHNE***)* I have your ring.

DAPHNE. Did you get that from Miriam?

HAROLD. Yes.

I am.

DAPHNE. You're what?

HAROLD. I – Miriam and I…

DAPHNE. *(realizing)* You…and Miriam…

NARRATOR. Just then, a doctor emerges to say, "I'm sorry."

DAPHNE. No, no, no, no, no, no, no, no, no....

(HAROLD *gets up to comfort her.* DAPHNE *stops him.*)

No!

(DAPHNE *runs out.*)

NARRATOR. Harold stays in the waiting room for a long time.

Midnight approaches and he walks outside.

As the night air hits his face, he freezes.

(HAROLD *stands. He doesn't know where to go.*)

After a moment, his feet begin to move.

(HAROLD *moves around the stage, lost. Eventually he stops walking and begins to sit down...*)

INSTANTS, MOMENTS
ONE FLICKERING FLAME OF LIGHT

ALL (NO HAROLD).

MMMMM
MMMMM...

NARRATOR. Instinct carries Harold to the stoop of his childhood home where he sits on the steps and stares at the sky for hours until –

[MUSIC #25: "NOVEMBER STARS"]

MR. MCCLAM. *(surprised)* Harold?

(MR. MCCLAM *sits down next to* HAROLD.)

Your mother's guitar...

(He picks the guitar up and looks at it.)

Y'know, don't laugh at me, but I think she was here tonight.

I think she saved my life.

With this blackout.

I don't believe in this kind of thing, normally, but tonight...

I know what you're thinking: "The old man's losing his marbles"...right?

MR. MCCLAM. *(cont.)* But she always liked blackouts.

I remember when you were little and there was a power outage in the building.

You were terrified of the dark.

You couldn't stop crying.

She sat with you for hours.

And that's when she invented her special trick.

Remember?

She'd hold her hand in front of your eyes, and tell you to stare straight at her palm. Then she'd tell you to count to ten.

*(**MR. MCCLAM** holds his hand up in front of **HAROLD**'s eyes and counts.)*

One, two, three, four, five, six, seven, eight...

HAROLD & MR. MCCLAM. Nine...ten.

MR. MCCLAM. And then she'd take her hand away and somehow...

Things looked a little brighter.

*(**MR. MCCLAM** takes his hand away and sees that Harold is crying.)*

Harold?

*(**HAROLD** hugs his father tightly.)*

Son? What's wrong?

HAROLD. I'm sorry.

*(**HAROLD** keeps hugging **MR. MCCLAM**.)*

*(After a beat, **HAROLD** stands to go. His father hands him his guitar and he takes it. He begins to walk around the stage once more.)*

(Music. The chorus sings.)

NARRATOR. Harold winds his way from Brooklyn to Manhattan.

Finally, he arrives at his fifth-floor walk-up apartment.

*(**HAROLD** climbs the steps.)*

And he's standing outside the door.

Not sure whether to go inside.

When he hears it.

(**HAROLD** *stops climbing.*)

Echoing down the stairs.

DAPHNE.
DEAR TINY DOTS OF TWINKLING LIGHT

NARRATOR. And so he climbs up to the roof.

(**HAROLD** *climbs to the roof and finds* **DAPHNE.**)

DAPHNE.
IT'S TIME FOR ME TO SAY GOODNIGHT
THERE'S SO MUCH MADNESS IN THIS WORLD BUT I FEEL
    SAFE

(*A beat.* **DAPHNE** *puts on her lucky ring.*)

'CAUSE I'M AWARE
YOU ARE UP THERE

NARRATOR. There's an invisible world woven into the fabric of our daily lives.

It may be impossible to fully comprehend.

But it *is* possible – I think – especially on those dark, dark nights…

When we feel afraid and lost and small.

To trust the connection. The connection to everything we *can* see.

HAROLD.
MMMMMM…

(**DAPHNE** *turns and sees* **HAROLD**. *They stare at each other for a beat.*)

NARRATOR. And to everything we can't.

DAPHNE. (*looking up*)
MMMMMM…

(**HAROLD** *looks up and moves toward* **DAPHNE.**)

HAROLD & DAPHNE.
OOOOOH…

(HAROLD begins to play his guitar.)

HAROLD & DAPHNE.
OOOOOH...
(Blackout.)

End of Show